If I Could Fly

JILL HUCKLESBY

EGMONT

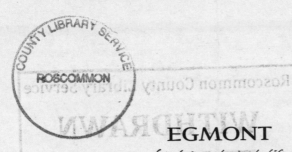

EGMONT

We bring stories to life

If I Could Fly
First published 2011
by Egmont UK Limited
239 Kensington High Street
London W8 6SA

Text copyright © 2011 Jill Hucklesby

The moral rights of the author have been asserted

ISBN 978 1 4052 5226 3

3 5 7 9 10 8 6 4 2

www.egmont.co.uk

A CIP catalogue record for this title is available from the British Library

Typeset by Avon DataSet Ltd, Bidford on Avon, Warwickshire
Printed and bound in Great Britain by the CPI Group

In memory of Zack, who walked eight thousand miles with me.

Chapter One

Thud and *thud* and stones and blood in mouth and mud and moon and stars and spikes of corn and trackies ripped and ribs on fire; ice sweat on neck and chest and spine and ache in calves and arms and eyes wide open, dry and cracked but dropping tears; there is no sound but feet, the snap of sticks, the rasp of autumn air in lungs, a pumping pulse of pain. Must keep the rhythm.

Om mani padme hum. Om mani padme hum.

Stream to cross, a leap, a thump, a bank to climb, a clutch at grass, a stile with broken step; the wood is wet with heavy dew and, here, a tarmac road to nowhere. Take me there. Please take me there. A place to hide, a space that's safe. My heart is pounding in my ears, a drum, a march, must stay in step, must hide my face in case they come, push my hair inside my hoody, keep

my head down, sprint and jog and sprint and jog.

No air . . . a stitch . . . a searing cramp. Eyes scan for cover. Beyond the hedge, a field, a tree with roots like fat man's legs a hundred metres up a slope, so thrust and push and elbows punch and eat the distance like it is the longest bacon sandwich in the world and munch and munch and holy mangoes! Made it.

Breathe. Stand still. Lean against the bark. Blend in. Don't cough. Shhh, heart. Don't beat so loud.

I have legs of stone. I'm a fugitive, on the loose. Memories of the last few hours are a blank computer screen in 'sleep' mode. I should be able to rerun them, like an HD game of escape at the touch of a button, and take myself back to the beginning. But the button is broken. All I remember is running down streets and alleys, across car parks, trading estates with perfect families smiling down from tattered billboards, a playground and a dual carriageway, watched by a dozen surveillance cameras, my trainers barely touching the ground.

What am I running from? My fist hits the gnarled wood behind me and sends an aftershock through my trembling frame. But it doesn't shake open the part of my brain that can answer the question. All it throws back at me is the last rule of the Phoenix Feathers, the gang of free runners on my estate: the rule I had to swear to obey if I wanted to learn their secrets; an oath sealed with spit from my throat and blood from my wrist; a vow broken, my brain tells me, without letting me access the facts. I feel in my gut it's the reason I am here, far from home, the faint taste of blood in my mouth.

Never trust a promise.

Chapter Two

Om mani padme hum.

It feels good to say the words. They mean: 'May there be peace and an end to suffering. May all be well.' It's my mum's daily prayer, before the dawn wakes the smiling Buddha who sits cross-legged in his tiny shrine on the windowsill in our kitchen. I call him Bud the Pud. My mum tells me I'm half Thai and should lay a respectful flower at his feet. She says that monks believe the chants' vibration alone can ease the troubles of the world. My dad says to her, 'Little Bird, your daily tweets are getting on my nerves.'

I sink down to my knees, leaning back against the tree's great trunk. The pain in my left side burns white hot. Its throb is like the tock of a clock, a ball against a wall, a hammer against a skull.

'The free runnin', it can save your life, Paper Clip,' Crease, the Phoenix Feathers' leader, told me, play-punching my shoulder. He's really fit, but it takes time for him to put words together. He never calls me by my real name. He says it ties his tongue in a knot just trying. So Calypso became 'Clip' and he added the 'Paper' as a tease. When he's tired, I become just plain PC. I'm always the butt of the gang's jokes, every which way.

I'm going to miss running with them – Crease and Slee and Moby, Jam and Shell, Foo and the others. Well, running behind them, technically, as I'm too young to be 'with' them, if you get me. I love hanging around when they train on the monkey bars, slides and suspended walkways in the playground near our estate, honing muscles, preparing for the next display.

'Watch and learn,' said Crease. And I did.

I remember watching them do a free run over our public library not long ago, when the nights first grew long and the air in our road smelled of sweet

honeysuckle. Their feet explored every wall, every angle, every ledge. But wait. Weren't there sirens and batons and shouting? Weren't Crease and Slee arrested? Didn't the rest of us vanish like sprites across the terraced rooftops and down thin alleys full of stinking rubbish? Wasn't there a whisper that the FISTS – the Forensic Investigation and Security Teams – had tracked them on all the social networking sites?

'You don't want to mess with the FISTS,' Foo told me later, dabbing at a cut on her cheek with the cuff of her fleece. 'Them and their "jaws on paws" sidekicks.' She shuddered and I saw her hand was shaking. We crouched by wheelie bins, waiting for the sound of raised voices to stop. When it was quiet, we scarpered over fences, through gardens, across roofs. When we reached the road, Foo pointed for me to go a different way. Swear to God, I saw her jump a parked car and disappear.

After that, I couldn't find the Feathers on any of

the usual online sites. My new mates had erased their profiles. And now, when I think of their features, framed by different coloured bandanas made out of tea towels, they are just a blur.

I rub my eyes, look up. In the sky, all I can see is a giant saucepan of fairy lights, hurtling my way. It's quite something when sparkly pans become lethal weapons with my name on.

Cal-yp-so (noun) – a folk song from the West Indies, maybe a story the singer makes up as she goes along.

'A girl with such a name is on a journey,' my mother would murmur in my ear, when I was small. 'She will have adventures. Her voice will be heard.'

Who will hear it now, Little Bird? Just night creatures – the rabbits, badgers and the mice. I daren't say it out loud, in case it's written on every news update to every curfew-centre computer in this region. It may already be travelling through cyberspace to the mobile phones of each officer patrolling the grid. I shouldn't be out here in the countryside. I don't have

permission to be travelling through areas zoned off by the quarantine.

It's a free country. That's what the graffiti in the shopping precinct says. Maybe it was, before the virus swept through and killed five thousand people. The government made a universal media announcement to explain that the virus is carried by wild animals, which must be kept out of the towns. Any found beyond the barbed-wire checkpoints are being destroyed. 'No great loss,' my dad said.

'Maybe it's all just a lie made up by the prime minister to keep everyone frightened,' I suggested to Crease.

'Maybe you should keep that thought to yourself, Paper Clip,' Crease had warned me, his eyes holding mine, unblinking.

'Free country,' I replied, deciding this would be my favourite phrase. Crease just shrugged, his sleek shoulders rising and falling like the curve of a mountain range. It made me feel hot and embarrassed, like there were weighty things I didn't get or understand. It was

a gesture that said, *You are just a kid — you know nothing.*

I thought, *Soon, when I'm fourteen, I'll know what you know.*

But look at me now. Crease was right. I'm just a kid without a plan. With a dodgy memory and stupid holes in my best trackies.

Forget Crease, I tell myself. Focus on this moment. The sit-u-a-shun, as the Feathers would say. Look around. Assess every contour. Map the footholds, ledges, flat tracks. Work out the next move.

It's funny. I was expecting things I've seen on the TV: endless coils of metal on the landscape, like giant Slinkies, blocking off the footpaths and the single-track country roads; signs with *Keep Out* in black and red; tape across farm gates; piles of dead sheep and cows; regular patrols by the FISTS. Maybe this zone is free from infection. Or maybe I just didn't see the warnings in the dark and this very moment the lethal 'glue' virus that makes your eyes stick together is spreading through every cell in my body. Maybe I've watched too

many movies and the moon's made of bendy cheese.

Do they know I've gone, Little Bird? You would never tell them, but there are others who might.

The facts will look like this – just words on a screen. Calypso Summer. Yeah, that really is my name. And then would come some letters. AAAR. Absent, alone and at risk. NYO. Not a young offender, unless you count the giant protest poster I stuck on the window of the discount clothes shop in the high street. Turned out its stuff is being made by kids younger than me, working twelve-hour shifts in complete dumps in India. It was my initiation act, to impress the Feathers. Crease took me to one side and kept repeating, 'Be cool at school, do you hear me? Break the System. Never get caught.'

Until I met Crease, I hadn't really thought much about the System. Life's OK on the estate, I thought. The gates don't bug me the way they bother some people. We have a two-bedroom semi with a nice white bathroom and our own garden with a pond. Our

kitchen is yellow and cheerful and smells of spices. There's a plasma TV; Dad insisted on that so he doesn't 'have to stare at the pictures of gold temples on the wall'.

I've got to keep focused. The ground beneath my feet is vibrating. There's a low thrumming close by, getting louder, the deep *whoop whoop whoop* of blades chopping through air. I throw myself face down and lie very still as a shaft of white light beams down into the field. Leaves are sucked into a swirl in the updraft. If this is a Wasp, the patrol helicopter of the FISTS, I'm in trouble. It feels like it's going to pull me skyward, chunk me up like a vegetable slicer.

I've seen Wasps on the TV. I know what they do. Any moment now, there will be a gush of liquid, the chemical solution they drop to stop the spread of the disease. The newsreaders say it's an anti-viral, but what if they're wrong? What if it's poison?

Are you looking for me? Is your sting ready?

My brain is in free fall.

Am I going to die, here, amongst worms and beetles and rotting leaves?

Everything is closing in. I'm imagining our front room – the grey sofas, the purple cushions with hand-stitched gold edging, the coffee table with elephant's legs made of wood. Then everything suddenly implodes. Little Bird becomes a tiny doll, standing amongst the rubble. Her smile is fixed and empty. Some huge force is propelling me away from her. I so want to feel the lightness of her touch, the softness of her fingers wrapping round my hand, as delicate as silk.

A wind rushes over the surface of my body. It feels as if it is stripping the clothes off my back. The thrumming instantly recedes. The Wasp is flying away, its luminous eye scouring the ground as it goes.

I'm on all fours, like a cat, trying to steady my eyes, which feel as if they are spinning in a vortex, and forcing back the waves of sickness washing up to my throat from my clenched gut.

I lie on my belly again, pushing my face into the

layers of damp leaf mould, letting the vegetation stifle a series of low moans which are spilling from my spleen, my liver, my lungs, my heart. In the tall trees, the rooks start to rasp in unison. In the dark undergrowth, the badgers shriek and the foxes howl.

I know what they are telling me. There is no going back.

Chapter Three

Daylight. I can tell, even though my eyelids are closed. I don't want to open them. It's not real, the soil on my tongue, this ache in my ribs, this burning in my thigh. Any minute now, Little Bird will open my door, wish me good morning and place a hot chocolate on my bedside table.

There are insects crawling over my face. I am frozen. My neck is stiff. There is no doubting now that my bed is the earth beside a massive, tangled tree root, and, when I dare to open my eyes, that my ceiling is a canopy of red-gold autumn leaves like giant hands, sheltering me. There are wood chips stuck on my cheek. Twigs digging into my chin. Dew is clinging to blades of grass like glass baubles and now, I am sucking at them, trying to rid myself of a terrible thirst.

Feelings of panic, hunger, fear and the need to pee come in waves. The pain in my thigh makes all of these fade into insignificance. I wish I could dissolve into the soil like the dew. Disappear off the face of the earth, like Foo.

I read that a child goes missing somewhere in the world every five minutes. Staying lost is another matter. That takes planning. As of a few hours ago, it wasn't at the top of my 'to do' list. I can't remember what was. Maybe if I ask myself some questions, the faulty bits in my memory will put themselves back together.

Where am I? Dunno. A field. The furthest from a Big Mac I've ever been.

Why am I running away? OK, brain, just give in and tell me!

Where am I heading? I'll come back to that one.

What will I do when I get there? Put up a flag, sing the national anthem, starve to death, how should I know?

What would you do, Crease? You wouldn't sit here feeling sorry for yourself.

So try again:

Where am I? Well, the sun is rising over there, so that's east. The hills at a sort of right angle to this tree must be south. That must be the direction I've been running in, because the Social Observation Tower is behind me, in the distance, like an upended barbecue skewer.

Why am I running away? Something happened, something that frightened me so much I took off and didn't stop.

Where am I heading? There are three choices, and it doesn't include phone a friend. I can go east, south, west. I need to find someone I can trust, or at least somewhere safe to hide out, preferably with a roof.

Concentrate, Caly.

It's like waiting to pull down the lever on a fruit machine, choosing the right moment to stop the circling pictures reeling in front of me. *Kerchunk-chunk-chunk.* Two bunches of grapes and a banana. Hey. It's not as random as it seems. That's the fruit Little Bird

16

brought me when I was in hospital three years ago, with appendicitis. And the hospital was on a hill near the sea. Maybe that's a good place to head. It felt safe there – maybe they can help me again?

What will I do when I get there? Maybe try to find the doctor with blond hair who told me jokes, and the nurse who gave me chocolate. Get some pain killers, clean clothes, food.

It's diddly squat, Paper Clip.

'It's a plan, Crease. I'd like to hear you come up with something better.'

I'm talking to myself. I do it all the time at school, really bums off the teachers. I don't mean to. The words just come out. It's odd because I'm quiet at home, careful. Dad doesn't like 'squawking' as he calls it – stupid chit chat. If he's not around, Little Bird and I have a good old gossip, but never raise our voices, just in case he comes through the door with one of his 'heads' on.

We like it when he goes upstairs, puts on those

eyepatches and stays in the dark, looking like a pirate, for hours until his migraine goes away. On those days, Little Bird and I cook a special tea of rice, chilli chicken and peanut sauce. She lights candles for the table and reads me the letters from my aunties and uncles in Thailand. She tries to explain the symbols that make up the words and giggles at my random guesses at translation. I'm not exactly fast when it comes to languages, but she says I am beautiful like a lotus flower, my petals unfolding. When I was born, she wanted to call me Padme, which means 'lotus', but Dad chose Calypso because it was the name of his first drink in the Caribbean when he worked in the Merchant Navy.

My gran says I'm a Heinz '57 – a mongrel not a pedigree. British but half Thai with almond-shaped eyes, wavy black hair and skin that tans as soon as it glimpses the sun.

I've looked up mongrels on Google. They are often stronger and healthier than pure breeds. Survivors, in

other words, who live on their wits, not their looks.

My wits are telling me I must get up and keep moving, using the cover of the woods, the long grass on open ground, the dense, spiky gorse bushes, anything I can find. It's dangerous, this daylight. All the rules are reversed now. It's only safe in darkness.

When I close my eyes for a moment, I can remember the smells of the hospital on the hill: the lemon hand-spray the nurses and visitors use before coming on the ward, the disinfectant in the corridors, the wood polish in the day room, the mouth-watering sweetness of cocoa from the vending machine. My tongue pokes through my cracked lips. I'm nearly swallowed up with anticipation.

It's time to shift.

Chapter Four

Stop running. Look around. Where am I now? Crouching low on a steep hillside. Sweat is trickling down my neck. My thigh is screaming. The pain is making me drowsy. I want to sleep, to sink into oblivion.

I've sprinted until my tank is empty, until my legs have crumpled, until the soles of my feet are raw with rubbed blisters.

Beneath me lies a flat plain of farmland, a patchwork of brown, gold and green squares with houses and barns dotted here and there like raised badger sets. Above is a sharp, grassy incline, rising so high that cotton-wool clouds seem to be balancing on the top. I hold my hand up and let one sit on my palm. If it was candyfloss, I could pluck it down and gobble it up. I

could eat the sky and then, maybe, the sun and have the moon for pudding.

I'd like to stay here until the end of time, in the warmth of the soil, and sleep. I'm drifting into my dream world, on a long-tailed speedboat, gliding between the giant rocks protruding from the azure Andaman Sea. My mother is next to me, wearing a wide wicker hat like an upturned lamp shade. When she laughs, beautiful red-whiskered bulbul birds fly from her mouth.

Sweet strains of music are whispering in my ears — the same melody, over and over. *La la, la-la la, la la, la-la la.* The sound is soft, distant, familiar. As the penny drops, I curl my knees over my chest and giggle.

An ice-cream van! I could be just a few minutes from a freezer full of lollies. I want to grab handfuls of them to hold against my skin and let their arctic coldness numb the burning in my thigh.

I'm running again, trainers scrabbling across bare patches of dry earth, and I'm stabbing my

of dry stalks, body bent forward as I scale the fierce incline. Up and up, eyes watering, nose running, I'm driven only by the thought of a release from pain.

'La la, la-la la,' I'm singing, and I don't care who hears. I'm almost there, the ridge at the top of the slope is just ahead. As I approach, my belly clenches. There's a wooden fence all along the perimeter, cordoned off with orange plastic mesh. A stile leading to a car park has security tape across its steps. I creep up to the barrier and stare through the square holes. There are no other cars here, no people to witness what I am about to do.

What am *I about to do? I haven't thought this through.*

The ice-cream man looks nice, kind even. If he's got kids of his own, maybe he would help me? More likely he would just haul me off to the police station and claim his reward for finding a runaway. And I would end up in the detention centre with no windows, where unruly kids are 'resocialised'. Crease says you get 'chipped' like a dog. The microchip they put in your

brain stops you being a 'threat to society' and lets the government know where you are, twenty-four seven. No one really knows what happens in the centre. The kids who get caught never talk about it later.

Surprise is the best form of attack. That's what Mr Thistle taught us about the English Civil War. Ice-cream Man won't be expecting a raid. The van's engine is running, so he won't hear me approaching. I can distract him, reach in and grab whatever I can.

He's wiping his counter with a cloth, his back turned to me. *Think like Crease, Moby and Foo.* I pick up a jagged flint and make a decision. It will take me five seconds to reach the van. No time to make a Plan B. Go, Caly!

I'm sprinting. I'm crouching next to the front tyre, ready to slip under the engine if necessary. I bite my lip so I don't cry out with the pain in my thigh. Tasting blood seems a regular occurrence these days. Maybe, come the full moon, I'll grow bushy eyebrows and long vampire teeth.

This isn't make-believe, it's war. And, for now, Ice-cream

Man's my enemy. I throw the rock as hard as I can up on to the roof of the van.

BANG BANG! It sounds like a coconut falling on to a corrugated hut, like a suitcase bumping down steps. It makes me cringe and cover my ears.

'What the . . . ?' Ice-cream Man has jumped out of the van and is looking up, taking off his baseball cap and scratching his head.

With the stealth of a leopard, I slink into the body of the vehicle, where the freezer is full of sweet treats. It's not food I want, but ice. I can't eat, no way. I need cold to dull the ache. Maybe then the horrible queasy feeling in my stomach will go away. In a nanosecond, I'm stuffing handfuls of lollies into my hoody and preparing to scarper.

There's a low rumble, the sound of an engine approaching, then a loud *woooo*. My brain struggles to match the sound to an image, then, suddenly, there's an information match. It's a patrol car. I crouch down as low as I can.

'Step away from the vehicle, sir,' I hear a man with a stern voice say.

'It's not illegal to sell ice creams. I've got a licence,' replies Ice-cream Man defensively.

'Please step away from the vehicle and put your hands in the air,' repeats Stern Voice.

'Give me a break!' retorts Ice-cream Man. The squeak of metal. Two car doors are opening. Footsteps.

'ID?' asks Stern Voice.

'In the van, with my licence.' I feel the vehicle rock slightly as Ice-cream Man gets into the driver's seat and reaches into a recess for his documents. I'm folding up as tight as a scrunched lolly wrapper, willing myself to be wafer thin, almost invisible, between two boxes.

'This is a prohibited public area until the excursion ban is lifted,' says Stern Voice. 'Didn't you see the signs?'

'Sorry,' apologises Ice-cream Man. 'Head in the clouds, me. They don't call me Mr Softie for nothing.'

There is no reaction from Stern Voice and his partner. Just a nervous laugh from Ice-cream Man.

Then, after a moment, 'Lucky for you your paperwork's in order, Mr Carter,' comments Stern Voice. 'We'll need to escort you back to town. Please follow the patrol car until we get to the green zone.'

'Wondered why there weren't any punters,' says Ice-cream Man – Mr Carter. 'Normally my busiest park-up. How long until the ban's lifted?'

'The Media Pod will advise the usual channels when the area's been swept,' replies Stern Voice. 'You'll get a text.'

Clunk, clunk. The car doors are closing again.

'I won't hold my breath, then,' says Mr Carter, putting the returned papers on the passenger seat. 'Excursion ban, my Aunt Norah,' he sighs, pushing the lever at his side into gear.

The van is moving. My escape route is closed off. Beads of sweat are trickling down my forehead.

Think logical, Paper Clip, I hear Crease say. *What are the positives? There's one, and it's staring you in the face.*

Yeah, that's true. I'm a prisoner, but I haven't been

caught. Like a rat, like a flea, I'm just hitching a ride. I'm going to jump to freedom, when the moment's right. When the world looks the other way, I'll be gone, right under the noses of the FISTS, like a feather on the wind.

'La la, la-la la,' says the van defiantly, like it's reading my mind.

Chapter Five

The smell of the ocean! We're slowing down now. I'm ready to jump ship, Cap'n Carter.

'On your way, then, boys,' Mr Carter says cheerily as a short blast of siren indicates that the official escort has ended. 'Back to fighting the drug dealers, murderers and fraudsters, now you've successfully prevented the public consuming ice cream on a weekday in an out-of-town car park. We're all safe in our beds, aren't we?'

I like Mr Carter. I think he's a bandit at heart. That's one of the best things to be, according to the Feathers.

'La la, la-la la,' sings the van, the sound harsher and more metallic now we're in town. We're slowing to a stop. The engine keeps turning over with a raw rumble. Mr Carter is making his way towards the counter in the back. I try to shrink even more, hoping he won't see

me sandwiched between the boxes underneath. Large hands reach down for a packet of cones. They are five centimetres away from my face. Which one of us will shout the loudest when he hauls me on to the worktop by mistake?

He is opening the sliding glass window. The sound of big children's voices assaults the space around me, like the screech of gulls fighting over fish.

'Good afternoon, and what's it to be, treasure?' Mr Carter says to the first in line.

'Choccy Mountain, please,' replies a young girl, in monotone. 'With all the stuff.'

'You must have a head for heights, young lady,' he says jokily. The ice-cream machine makes a deep gurgling, slurping noise, like my gran with a bowl of soup, before she forgot how to feed herself.

'I'm going to eat it, not climb it,' the girl responds, bored.

'Sarcasm costs extra,' says Mr Carter.

'It says the toppings are free,' whines the girl.

I would laugh out loud, if my sit-u-a-shun was not so serious.

Why are you waiting, Caly? The moment is NOW!

Before you can say 'mischievous macaque monkey', I'm shooting from my hidey-hole like a bullet from a silenced gun. I'm out of the van and away down a street I've never seen before. A street full of parked cars and colourful terraced houses with balconies, running parallel to the sea. My escape is just as I hoped – so fast, no one has seen me. Only the big yellow bug eye in the sky, which doesn't even blink.

I cross the road at a sprint and extend the distance between me and the queue of ice-cream teens. I hope Mr Carter's not too angry when he discovers that he has mysteriously misplaced a box of Rainbow lollies. *Tea-leaf, tea-leaf, tea-leaf THIEF!* This isn't a skipping game in a playground, I tell my conscience. No way. It's about survival.

It's unnerving, the buildings and cars and traffic, the

feeling of pavement underfoot and the stench of rubbish spilling out from over-filled wheelie bins. In the countryside, I turned feral to survive. In this urban wilderness, my senses feel overloaded. There are so many predators here. Some of them are not even human – CCTV could capture me with one flash. I must stay off the main roads, at all costs.

I'm sprinting, checking left and right for an opening into an alley, where a kid who looks as beaten-up as me can hang out until dark. Nothing doing, just rows of steps up to grand entrances and down to basement flats. I choose the most unloved-looking building, covered in a creeping plant, and slip down stone stairs to a dark porch obscuring a door whose paint is peeling off and whose letter box is missing.

I sit on the bottom step, rip open the box of lollies and hold a handful against my thigh. I need a bath full of ice, but this will have to do. The cold makes my skin tingle. After a few minutes, numbness replaces pain. My tongue is dry but I don't feel thirsty, just so tired.

A tabby cat with yellow eyes is staring down at me between the wrought-iron railings above. It rubs its face against the black bars and I can hear it purring. I'd give anything to be that cat, perfectly content in the sunshine.

Looking through the gaping hole in the door, the place looks empty: there's a carpet of junk mail on the floor, dirty net curtains hang limply at the two windows, empty fast-food boxes are abandoned on the narrow terrace. I hunker on my calves, hug my knees, my back against the wall of the steps. It will be hours until it's dark, but I must keep hidden, even though it smells like a toilet down here.

Above, the *click, clack, click, clack* of kitten heels, the *bam bam bam* of a ball being bounced, the *week, week, week* of a squeaky tyre on a bike or buggy as it's pushed along. Although I am only a metre away from them, I am invisible, like a rat in a sewer. But I will surface again. This is not my last resting place, amongst the rubbish and the climbing ivy and the giant spider's web

that stretches from the window to the wall.

It's just my hidey hole where I've decided to hang out and let the pain in my thigh calm down. I know there's no escape route, Crease — nobody's perfect. And I'm only going to close my eyes for a minute because I'm watching the gulls gliding in a circle and it's making me sleepy. Shhh.

Chapter Six

The ground under my body is vibrating. I'm a sheet being jiggled to take out my folds. Is that thunder, rumbling closer? I open my eyes. They begin to focus on cracked concrete and tangled ivy. An old, wizened face (a man, a woman who has lost her hair?), peering at me, net curtain drawn to one side. A disfigured hand beckoning to me, pointing to the front door.

I feel like screaming, but no sound comes. One, two, three, I'm counting drops of water hitting the ground – that's not good – and now the sky is falling in and I'm almost winded by the force of the water pelting down into the narrow basement, soaking me through.

The face has gone. Has it been there all the time, watching me? Did I imagine it? Fear has jumbled my

responses. Dare I look through the gaping mouth in the door?

I tilt my head back and try to drink but the drops have turned to ice, hitting my skin like pebbles on glass. No part of me is dry. No part of me wants to stay in this dark, wet hole. My legs are moving before my brain even clocks the sliding of the bolts and the creak of hinges opening very slowly. My hip bone feels as if it is grinding against gravel. The pain is making me feel sick, but I can't give in to it.

Up, up, up the steps, in three leaps, back on to the pavement. No one sees me. I'm invisible in the rain, a drowned rat scurrying, head down.

Flash flash BANG! The sound and light show has begun. The town looks like a film set for a moment, illuminated by a hundred arc-lamps, with a rain machine on full tilt. Spouts of water three metres high are spurting from storm drains.

I want someone to say 'Cut!' and to take me into a trailer full of warm towels, hot milk and a huge plate of

chilli chicken with rice, to dry my hair and wrap me in the softest cotton robe you can buy.

I want Little Bird to hold me and tell me everything's all right.

I don't want to be sheltering in a pub doorway, waiting for the deluge to end. My clothes are steaming, my eyes are streaming. Not tears. My dam has burst. The water has to flow out somewhere.

A man with a ring through his cheek and a woman with studded eyebrows and black eyes appear out of the mist, walk past me with disinterest and push open the pub door. I glimpse customers at tables, tucking into fish and chips or lasagne. They look happy. I feel even more alone. The door swings shut before anyone inside can raise an eyebrow at the kid who is loitering, looking lost.

What's your plan, Paper Clip?

I'll keep moving, Crease. Like you said, a moving target is harder to hit.

I'm running through rainbows. The wall of water

has become a fine mist shot through with sunlight. Richard Of York Gained Battle In Vain. Gran taught me that to help me remember the colours of the arc. She makes a wish whenever she sees one. I'm panicking, trying to think of the best thing to wish for. It's no good – I can't think clearly and sprint at the same time.

Come on, brain, help me work out what to do next. I need to get to the hospital. Let's just focus on that, OK? My thigh feels like it's being attacked by a meat slicer. How did I get injured? Did it happen when I ran away? Is it something to do with the Feathers? Why did I take off with no money, no phone, no ID, no plan? It would help if you could stop your little game and tell me what happened. Just give me a clue – anything.

Glimpses of bright blue sea are winking at me as I splash across roads, kerbs awash with overflow water from the drains. I'm heading west, I think, towards the setting sun and the hill in the far distance. I remember the view from the hospital ward where I was treated.

It looked down over the town to the sea. This has to be the right direction.

I need to be vigilant. Now the rain has eased up, there will be patrol cars out and about again and the CCTV cameras will have a clear view.

'Life can turn on a five-pence piece,' Gran says. I never really understood what she meant until now. When things start spinning, they can go face up or down. Less than a day ago, I was a kid with a routine. I knew what to expect. Days were a blur of school, homework, thinking of new ways to avoid the electronic ID scan by the gates of our estate. At night, there would be Mum's exotic stories of elephants and strange fish, and monkeys that steal food, clothes and trinkets from the night markets in Chang Mai. It didn't matter that Dad wanted the TV and the whole front room to himself. We were happy, just the two of us.

Maybe I didn't realise someone had flipped the coin and that things were in the balance. *'Mai pen rai'* – no worries! – Mum always said, no matter what happened.

Not long ago, though, I found her crying. She said she felt like the tiny Thai birds captured in nets so that they could be released during festivals. They were never truly free.

I told Mum about the Feathers; how they could scale almost any man-made barrier in their way, how they had this amazing agility. She smiled and asked if she were too old to join.

And she told me to be careful, because some people didn't agree with that kind of crazy running without rules, even though this is a free country.

Chapter Seven

I've arrived in the Magic Kingdom, swear to God. In this part of town the buildings are like toy houses, leaning against one another, with chimneys and front doors all in a line and every colour you can think of. The road rises steeply and curves, coils, snakes back and forth. The castle-shaped towers at the top are raised high above the long brick structure beneath, under a deep pink and orange sky.

Any moment, there could be fireworks . . .

I don't remember the hospital looking like this. Then again, when you're clutching your belly and a bucket in turn, you don't notice detail, just pain. Even if Snow White herself had appeared with the seven dwarfs, whistling a happy tune, she couldn't have made me smile.

A church clock struck six a while ago. The sun is just a red crescent, sinking into the sea. The air smells of salt and wood smoke, incense sticks and uncollected refuse. Gulls the size of terrier dogs are picking at abandoned black sacks on the pavement, spreading their contents with yellow beaks.

Almost there. The hill is so steep my legs feel as if they are moving in slow motion. The windows are blazing in the last rays of light. This close, the hospital is less like a fairy castle and more like a fortress. I had forgotten the huge wall round its perimeter and the giant stone griffins standing on high pillars either side of the gateway to the main entrance. They have the bodies of lions and their eagle heads are thrown up in a massive roar.

Holy hummingbirds, something is terribly wrong here. There are boards saying *Keep Out, Private Property* across the drive. There must be a mistake. A hospital never turns patients away. As my eyes scan the upper segment of the building, I notice that some of the

windowpanes are broken or missing and there's ivy creeping under the roof gables. It has an air of neglect, like a corpse left behind on the battlefield, a casualty of war.

Look at the problem every which way, Paper Clip; the size of the barriers, the angle needed for your ascent.

I'm jogging with heavy feet along the perimeter of the wall, hoping for an opening, an explanation, a welcome. I'm greeted by streams of black and red graffiti tags, locked doors and high metal gates chained together. I wrap my fingers round the cold bars and rest my head against them, exhausted.

'No, no, no, no, NO,' I'm saying, over and over again, in disbelief. My arms are wrenching at the gates, which make a clanking noise like a metal monster yawning, but barely move.

I'm staring into the overgrown garden where three swings suspended from a wooden frame sway in the breeze, bumping into one another aimlessly. A rocking-horse head with grab bars has fallen off its spring and

lies amongst the wild grass. Two benches lie smashed and in pieces. On a third sits a small teddy, holding a red heart. His fur is grey with dirt. His eyes are fixed in my direction, unblinking. A shiver ripples down my body from my skull to my toes. It is so unexpected, I bite my tongue.

For some crazy reason, I want to hold the bear. I scan the road, up and down. No vehicles. No pedestrians. Only the greedy gulls peck, peck, pecking. I move back to the wall, which is about three metres high and has a ledge at the top. This would be a classic manoeuvre for the Feathers involving just three actions, so here goes:

1. Jump up from a standing position, grabbing the ledge
2. Pull up and anchor my body with a foot on the ledge
3. Roll or swing over the top of the wall, landing silently

OK, not exactly silently, but I've done it! Easy peasy lemon squeezy, even if I have grazed my left hand and twisted my right ankle almost out of its socket. Crease would have scaled the wall almost without touching it, but, hey, he's Phoenix Alpha.

I'm crouching low, checking the terrain. Red tape cordons off the grassy area in front of the main entrance. The remains of large cardboard boxes and several piles of old blankets are spread out behind it. Cans of drink are lined up against the side of the hospital's wall and a bare rose bush is wearing a man's jacket, bent low under the weight.

The grounds are a mess, the tarmac driveway breaking up under pressure from weeds pushing through from the earth below. Information signs have been removed, leaving only the metal poles they were attached to.

A lot of the windows I'm looking at now are boarded up. One of the boards even has a neat painting of a blond kid waving from inside a window.

Artist joker! Must have taken ages to do. It looks quite spooky.

There's no one about, hardly any sound, just the distant thrum of traffic from the town and an occasional *rawk-rawk* of a seagull, flying overhead. I move cautiously towards the bench and its lone inhabitant, ready to run if there is so much as a whisper of danger.

The bear looks smaller up close. I sit next to him and lift him on to my lap. He is still wet from the rain. His eyes are scratched and misty. When I squeeze his heart, he says, 'I love you,' in a funny voice.

'I love you too,' I reply, and give him a kiss on his damp head. He smells of wood and leaves, of night air and soggy stuffing.

'You need a name, bear,' I tell him, looking into his face. 'You look like you were once fluffy, but now your fur is matted and flat. The seams of your paws are coming undone. You should go to teddy hospital. Maybe you came here, just like me, thinking they would

make you better. Easy mistake to make. I think we're not allowed to be sick any more, bear, that's the truth. The doctors and nurses have vanished –'

'My name is Andy. I just *lerve* honey.'

'How did you do that? I didn't press anything! So, you're called Andy, are you? That's a nice name for a bear. I'm Calypso, Caly for short.' I take his paw in my hand and give it a shake. 'Nice to meet you.'

Andy doesn't respond, just stares at me with unseeing eyes. I hold him close, his heart against mine. I can feel mine beating very fast. I can also feel a numb ache spreading up my legs and around my hips. All my energy seems suddenly to have left my body, and whooshed away amongst the scattering autumn leaves. I'm as floppy as a rag doll. If I sit here much longer, that's what I'll become.

'Shall we stay or go, Andy?' I ask him. 'What's that? You're thinking about it. Yeah, well, one of us has to make a decision. It's cold out here. It's nearly dark. There's nowhere else to head for tonight. We could

sleep inside, out of the wind and rain, and make a new plan tomorrow. What do you say?'

There is a strange hiccupping, buzzing noise from Andy. It's a response, at least. I take it as a 'yes'.

'Here goes, then,' I say quietly, poking the bear down the front of my hoody, in case I need to run. I move towards the front of the huge, derelict building, checking for possible entry points. Even though it looks like it doesn't want visitors, I'm drawn to the main entrance – a vast door with cylindrical stone pillars either side. I can see my reflection in the long, thin windows. I'm shocked by how much of an urchin I look.

I stop, take a deep breath. Everything is eerily quiet. Having Andy close is giving me courage, though. Crazy idea, Caly. It's not like he's a kung fu black belt, or anything useful. I walk up the three shallow steps to the entrance. This is how Alice must have felt in Wonderland. The door is so huge I imagine I am shrinking, shrinking. Soon I won't be able to reach the big brass handle.

Cut it out, brain. Behave.

I walked through this entrance once before, only then there was light and bustle and the smell of antiseptic, and flowers on the reception desk and colourful mobiles of sea creatures hanging from the high ceiling above a wide staircase with a polished wooden hand rail. It's like it was yesterday. I close my eyes and imagine I am holding Little Bird's arm, that Dad is parking the car, that there is a bed in a pale-green ward waiting for me, that soon my problems will be over.

I feel dizzy. My vision spins with images of roaring griffins, laughing nurses, a doctor with a syringe, Little Bird crying, Andy saying, 'I love you,' over and over again. I'm falling, and my thigh is tense with pain, but as I reach out to grab the handle of the door so that I can steady myself, I realise I'm experiencing a memory. A moment later, it is gone and the agony subsides.

What was that, brain? Something from my past or a malfunction?

Confused and shaken, I lean against the door. There is a loud creaking and it begins to give way, opening heavily on to a tiled floor, strewn with envelopes.

Suddenly, there's a terrible screeching noise. I put my hands over my ears just as a huge dark shape, as big as a vulture, swoops out of the darkness inside, the draught from its wings ruffling my hair as it passes. It is a raven, ragged and probably starving. *How long has it been trapped in here?* It is so close to my face I look into its eye. There is just a socket, scratched raw by claws.

Someone is screaming. I think it's me.

Chapter Eight

It's like the rainforest in the stories you've read me, Little Bird. Full of unknown dangers. Look! Tangled wires like tendrils hanging from a high canopy. *Waay!* Are there monkeys here? And what about those curled-up cables, like coiled snakes? Will they unravel and attack if I step inside?

I'm looking in with eyes narrowed against the failing light. My legs feel like jelly. I'm so tired. So tired of being tired. So tired of the pain in my leg.

A hundred questions hurtle into my head as I hover half in and half out of the jungle of weeds growing up through the floor. Why was the door open? Was it a mistake by the security company whose name is on the board by the road? Does it mean someone will be back to check? Are there regular patrols, maybe with dogs?

It's no good. The thoughts are tumbling now as fast as a waterfall's torrent. I don't have any answers. All I know is I can see my breath steaming like vapour from a kettle. That means one thing. Night is coming. I need somewhere to shelter.

My legs jerk and carry me forward. I'm inside and looking up at the domed ceiling from which a sad, grey bulb hangs like a nose drip on the end of a long cable.

Plip, plip, plop. Somewhere, a tap is leaking. The sound echoes eerily amongst the empty corridors leading away from the hallway. I'm passing the closed metal door to the lift and slowly ascending the staircase, fingers lightly resting on the dusty wooden rail, eyes straining against the gloom, feet almost arching up on my toes, ready to take flight at the drop of a hat.

Nobody drops hats any more, Paper Clip, you know what I'm sayin'? Keep your eyes open for any kind of dodgyness.

'Yeah, I know what you're saying, Crease. Trouble is, there's so much dodgyness it's hard to know where to begin.' I'm whispering back to the shadows,

which is really lame, scaring myself with the sound of my own voice.

I've reached the first-floor landing. My eyes do a sweep, first left, then right, down the empty corridors where kids like me used to pad about in dressing gowns and slippers. Opposite, there should be two glass-panelled doors leading to Wonderland Ward. There is just a space. The sign above the doorframe is still there, although part of it is missing. I can just make out the letters. Now it just reads *Wonderland*.

Nothing could look further from the truth.

'Do you believe in fairies?' the ward sister had asked me when I arrived, all that time ago. It was a strange thing to say to someone whose face was staring at the inside of a bucket. I think I must have nodded, because then she said, 'You can come in,' and she showed me to a bed by the window which had a pink duvet cover. There was a row of books on the tiled sill, held up by two wooden owls either end.

Today, Wonderland is just a long, rectangular space,

empty but for a single armchair at one end. There are eight floor-to-ceiling windows that look out over the overgrown garden below. Light from the streetlamps is filtering in through the dusty panes like pointy fingers, accusing me of a crime.

Yes, I ran away, and I'm so sorry, Little Bird, for all the pain that's causing you.

As I walk over the bare floor, my steps echo – or is it my heart I can hear? I give Andy a squeeze. He is silent. I take him out of his hiding place and show him the spot where I once lay sick and frightened, hitched up to a tube.

'I had a nice view of the garden, look,' I say to him, holding him up to the window. His hard nose leaves a hole in the dust. He is limp and unresponsive in my hand.

'I get it. You're an "I don't care" sort of bear,' I say, cleaning him up and putting him back inside my hoody. *Or maybe you're really scared, just like me.*

My feet are carrying me forward again, like a sleep

walker, like a drone, like a zombie. I'm approaching the chair, which seems as good a place as any to rest for a while and maybe, later, to drift off into the kind of sleep when you have one eye open, looking for dodgyness.

The chair has wide arms and a low back covered in old dark blue velvet. Its seat is thick and inviting and when I fall back into it there is a *foof* as a cloud of dust rises from its worn fabric. It makes me cough and almost gag, especially when I remember that the particles swirling around me are almost ninety per cent skin. Skin from the hundreds of children who were nursed back to health here. I don't want to think about the ones who didn't make it. Have their souls stayed behind, to keep watch? I don't believe in that stuff, honest to God, but it feels like there are eyes watching me from the darkness and shadows moving between the dust as it falls.

Sprites and ghosts, ghouls and vampires. They all seem possible in the night. *Keep it real, Paper Clip*, Crease would say. And he would probably tell me to *Sit in the*

chair, make a plan and stop crying. You got yourself into this mess. You can get yourself out of it.

Did I? I could never have chosen this, never in a month of Sundays. And if they catch me? They will alter my brain. Game over.

My thoughts are jumbled, like a stir-fry of noodles and peppers, twisting together, a mass of slippery strands. The pain in my thigh is burning like chilli in your eyes. The more you rub, the worse it gets. But the chair is soft and is letting me sink into it. It's the nearest thing to a hug I've had for a long time. I realise how much I'm longing for that safe feeling of being held; to be so close to another heart you can hear its beat.

I miss you, Mum. There are reasons why I am here and you are there. I will remember. I will understand. And maybe that's the day I will be able to come home.

I've rested here long enough. I'd like to sleep but pangs of pain are jabbing their spears into my belly. It's so hard to move. I've morphed into the squishy seat. It's sucking me into its springs and padding. My eyelids

are heavy and my head is starting to loll. Grip the arms and count to three, then stand up – good plan. Here goes. One, two . . .

'WHAT ARE YOU DOING IN MA CHAIR? YES, *YOU*, CHOP SUEY!'

Chapter Nine

There is no time to move. The man who shouted is standing over me. His face is so close to mine I can smell the onions on his breath and see the peppermint whites of his eyes. His dark hair hangs in straggles across his face. Under the black plastic sheet that covers his frame, I can see layers of clothes – at least two shirts and a jumper. His trousers are held up with green string. Wafts of old sock assault my nostrils. But there's another smell lingering underneath – something unexpected but familiar.

'I said, what are you doing in ma chair?' he repeats slowly, threateningly.

'Sitting,' I reply truthfully. *Idiot, Caly. You broke the rule. You got caught.*

'I didna give you permission to sit in ma chair.' The

man grabs my arms and pulls me upwards. The force of it sends me spinning into the wall. 'Next time, you have to ask,' he growls, smoothing out the velvet on the seat.

'Sorry,' I reply, stunned. You should be polite to crazy people, Gran says, because you never know what they're going to do next. There are different types of crazy, though, from mad axe men to nice people who have lost their marbles.

'Are you hurt?' he asks, noticing me rubbing my elbow. The tone of his voice is softer now, kinder.

'It's nothing.' I'm working out my chances of escape. If I run, can I make it to the stairs, flip over the banister and drop to the ground floor without breaking every bone in my body? Crease and Slee could do it. But I'm just a stupid kid, with no easy way out.

'So you decided to crash my pad, then, Chop Suey?' the man accuses.

'I didn't know it was yours,' I reply carefully. 'And I'm not Chinese, if that's what you think. I'm Thai. Well, half, anyway.'

'You are, are ye?' he says, walking towards me. 'Little Miss Saigon, eh?'

I don't want to tell him that Saigon is in southern Vietnam, a totally different country. And that its proper name is Ho Chi Minh City. My neck is flushing hot with indignation and fear.

'Ma pad, that's correct. And if you want to share it there'll have to be some rules, savvy?' he says matter of factly.

I feel as if I'm on a treadmill and the moving panel beneath my feet is accelerating faster and faster so that my legs won't keep up. I wasn't going to stay here – only for one night – but if he's not Mad Axe Man crazy, is it such a bad idea? Just until I'm stronger? Just until I've worked out where I'm going?

'OK, what are the rules?' I ask, playing for time. Even in the semi-light, I can see him swallow heavily and rock backwards on his trainers, which, I notice, don't match. Ha! So, there are no real rules, just the ones he's about to make up.

'Number one,' he begins. 'You don't sit in ma chair without permission and never in the morning when I'm reading the paper.'

'You get the paper?' I ask warily. There's only one daily now, published by the Office of Media and Communications, and photos of missing kids are always run in a banner across the centre pages with a reward offered for information.

'With ma chips,' he replies. 'I like the crosswords. But don't interrupt, do you hear, Miss Saigon?'

'I'm Calypso,' I state. I've had it with nicknames, especially ones that aren't even geographically correct. 'That's what you should call me. And what should I call you?' I demand, keeping my voice low and even, like Little Bird when she is soothing my dad's 'niggle niggle' – the temper he comes home with after visiting the social club and discussing 'the state of things' with the crowd there.

'My name's Dair. Dair McFarlane,' he replies, giving me a little salute as an afterthought.

'Cool,' I say, which sounds a bit ridiculous in the circumstances. Neither of us moves. There is an awkward silence. 'So, rule number two?' I prompt. Dair looks confused for a moment, as if telling me his name has let the cat out of the bag.

'Ay, rule number two,' he nods. 'I live in Willows Ward next door, but ma chair needs space around it, so you can have that half of Wonderland Ward,' he tells me, waving a finger at the space at the end of the room.

'Why can't you just move the chair next door?' I ask logically.

'Look, Little Miss Clever Chopsticks – the chair stays exactly where it is. You don't touch it, you don't move it, you don't put your person in it, you don't take any kind of liberty with it at all, ever. Do you understand me?' His voice is harsh suddenly and he's pacing up and down in front of me, like an army major reprimanding his troops.

I nod, observing him, recalculating my escape plan, in case things go bad in the next few moments. I'm not

fully focused, though. There's a distraction. That sweet, surprising aroma again. My brain won't connect with the clues my nose is giving it.

'Rule three,' he continues, speaking faster than before. 'Everything is to be neat and tidy at all times. Including the bathroom. No clothes left draped or dripping. No food containers or remains – or the rats will be your bedfellows and feed on your eyeballs. Above all, no hair on the floor or in the plughole of the sink.' I can see his shoulders shudder. 'There will be regular inspections and anyone, that means you, breaking these rules will be disciplined by the judge, that means me, and punished.'

That's it. Crazy or not, he's got it coming.

'You're not in charge of me,' I point out boldly. 'You can't order me about, just because I'm a kid. We don't need to have anything to do with each other. We don't even have to speak. This isn't your pad. It's a derelict hospital. You've broken in, just like me. We're the same: outlaws. There are three floors and about

a dozen rooms to choose from. I don't even need to be in the same place as your precious chair. I'm going to sleep downstairs, as far away from you as possible. Tomorrow I'll probably be gone, because this isn't what I planned. It's not what I came here for. I wanted nurses, the kind doctor and some painkillers. I've got to get better, so I can remember. I have to, do you get me? Because otherwise, I can't –'

'Here y'are,' Dair is saying, motioning me to approach him. 'No, come on, I won't bite – grrrrrrr – no, really, I'm joking you.' Something in his manner is persuasive. I'm about to burst into tears. I want to respond. Tentatively, I move towards him. He puts his hands lightly on my shoulders and swivels me gently, easing me down into the chair.

'Rest your heed,' he says, crouching close by and staring at me with a worried expression. 'I didna mean all those things I said. Except about the chair, OK?' I make a motion to rise but Dair shakes his head. 'I'm making an exception,' he explains, 'this once, mind.'

'It's a nice chair,' I say, all fight spent.

'It is, that's a fact,' Dair agrees, stroking the velvet arm. 'Can ye keep a secret?' he whispers, gazing into my eyes.

'Um, yeah,' I shrug.

He motions for me to lean closer. 'I'm a wanted man.'

'Why?' I ask.

'Bonny Calypso, mate, it's not that hard. Look at me. What do you see?' Dair stands up in front of me and struts about.

I'm searching for words that won't offend him.

'Yes, I can see what your wee brain is thinking. I'm dangerous, me. I'm an anarchist, at war with the System. I'm gonna bring it down and set the people free!' Dair punches the air with his fist.

'That's your secret?' I'm not totally impressed.

'Noooo. I'm really the president of Asia. Of course it's my secret. And now it's yours too.' He is pointing a dirty finger at me. 'Do ye want to be a freedom fighter wi' me?'

I shrug again.

'Well, you cannot. Not without training. And there's no time for that.' Dair begins to walk towards the open doorway.

'Where are you going?' I ask.

'On a mission. Wait.' He hurries back and presses a small metal object into my hand. 'Look after this. Guard it.'

'It's a bottle top,' I say.

'Shh. What are ye thinking, even saying its name?' Dair has a finger to his lips. 'This is the key to everything.'

'I don't understand,' I tell him.

'It opens the security door to the Hive, the government computer centre. It's where all the information on every citizen is stored, where all the CCTV cameras are linked up to, where all the young offenders' microchips are programmed.' Dair is rubbing his left temple thoughtfully.

'Why do you want me to look after it?' I ask him.

'Ye are a blitherer, do you know that?' he sighs. 'I can't take it on ma mission, can I?'

'Why not?'

'Because if they find it they will know, and the whole operation will be blown.' He raises his eyes to the ceiling.

'Who are *they*?'

'The FISTS,' replies Dair. 'I've been fighting them since I was fifteen. Since they took ma –' He strides away quickly, leaving the word unsaid. 'So, what's it to be, Chop Suey?' he calls from the landing.

'Yes,' I reply.

'Whaddya mean?'

'Yes, I'll keep your secret.'

'That wasne what I was asking ye,' says Dair, exasperated. 'Will ye be wanting fish, or a pie, with chips? Does no one in this place know their own mind?'

'I'm not hungry,' I tell him. The pain in my thigh is suddenly throbbing like a hammer on a molten horseshoe.

'Suit yerself. I won't be long. There'll be three knocks when I'm back so you know it's me and you can open the door.' And with that he is gone. I can hear the thud of feet descending the stairs and a deep clunk as the heavy door closes behind him.

My heart is still racing. Now I am alone again, none of the events of the past few minutes seem real. Is Dair a figment of my imagination? Have I conjured him up because I'm so tired my brain is out of control? The bottle top in my hand answers both questions.

The things Dair said don't add up. This metal disc is clearly not a key. But the stuff about the Hive – I've heard that name before, from Crease. And it makes a shiver travel down my spine.

'The FISTS don't like sit-u-a-shuns they can't control, Paper Clip,' he told me. 'And kids who climb like monkeys and leap like cats spook them. The Phoenix Feathers is not on the official list of running clubs, you get me? It's on another list – freedom fighters. They think free runners are enemies of the

System. There are a hundred eyes in the Hive watching me, watching you. Watching your family. They can zoom right in. Identify you. So cover your face and move like the wind.'

Suddenly I see myself sprinting down the passage which links my street to the trading estate at the back of our house. It is dark and hard to see. Even so, my feet are almost flying over the ground. It's just a flash of memory. My body shudders in response and it feels like fire is licking at my thigh.

Nothing else, brain? No other clue? Just a cold sensation in my stomach, the realisation that I'm not just a runaway, but an enemy of the System. A MISYO – Missing Young Offender. So it's not just me the FISTS will be trying to capture and recondition. It could be my family too. I must warn Little Bird somehow, but right now the thought of going back makes my mind freeze with fear.

Chapter Ten

'Keep it straight, mate, or I'll look like a pair o' black-out curtains.'

Dair is sitting in his chair with his back to me, staring at himself in the mirror I found this morning. It is cracked in two places, but only in the corners. He said it was 'a perfect find'. His dark eyes seem surprised by what they see. He keeps turning his head left then right to look at his profile. My scissors are poised and I'm already regretting offering to cut his unruly locks.

'Well, are ye going to hairdress or nay?' he's asking.

'I am,' I reply. I mean, how hard can it be? A straight line across the back is all it needs. He doesn't want me messing with the front or putting layers in, thank goodness. I've brushed it out ready and it's still damp after being washed, so here goes.

Snip. The first tuft falls to the floor. It's not a clean cut. The scissors I found in Dair's tool collection are quite blunt.

'That's half ma heed, you blitherer,' he complains.

'It's an inch, like you asked for. Stop complaining or go to a salon.' My face is hot with tension. The sweet smell my nose now associates with Dair – the smell I'd noticed that first day – wafts into my nostrils. Whoever thought of putting mangoes into shampoo was a genius. My eyes sting a little as my head is bombarded with memories of Little Bird slicing a juicy fruit in half in our kitchen at home, turning the skin inside out and cutting away the chunks of fruit. I'll be glad when Dair finishes his supply and starts the Ocean Silk instead.

He washes his hair every day. It's a kind of obsession. The floor in his bathroom is lined with plastic containers – every kind of brand name – and each one is about half full. There are conditioners too. Dair takes them from wheelie bins before the bags are collected and then tops them up with water.

The heavy mass I'm trying to tame is shoulder length and black as ink, with a gentle wave. It hasn't been cut for a long time and there are lots of split ends.

'I'm watching paint dry here,' Dair sighs. From time to time, he takes the special bottle top from his coat pocket, just to check it's there, then puts it back.

'You try creating an edge with wallpaper scissors,' I snap. When I glance in the mirror, Dair is smiling. That's the first time since we've met. I pretend not to have noticed. I don't feel like being chummy, even though I sense he is beginning to like me a little.

He's still got his stupid rules. I'm not allowed in his bathroom, which is along the corridor from Wonderland, and is much nearer than the other one he's allocated me. I've been keeping clear of his precious chair, natch. I like my own space anyway, and it's starting to look like home. It's amazing what you can find in skips and bins around the town. Every day, on my hunting expeditions, I've come back with books, clothes, small tables, a flower vase, a chair, cushions,

a yoga mat, even a mattress. I have to help myself to things when there's no one around to see me and wonder what I'm doing.

I'm piling the books up to create makeshift rooms in my half of the ward, and so far I've got two pillars of paperbacks for a front door, half a bedroom and the foundations for a lounge. I'm trying to stick to a theme for each area – cookery books for the kitchen, interior design manuals for the sitting room and novels for my sleep space, which is looking quite cosy with a purple throw over the mattress and the cushions on top. Most of the books that people throw out are about gardening, but I don't really need those. They might be good fillers, like the mortar between the bricks, if I get desperate.

There's a scare about growing flowers and vegetables. The government says the virus might be in the soil. Every day there are queues outside the supermarkets that stock produce from other countries. No one wants home-grown food now, just in case.

Farmers are going out of business and letting their cows and sheep loose to roam through towns. Dair said he saw a bull trotting through a graveyard yesterday, but it was probably one of his tall stories. He also said cows roam around everywhere in India, because they are sacred. I asked him how he knew that – had he been there and seen the Taj Mahal? Did he think it was one of the Seven Wonders of the World? He told me to keep 'my piggy nose' out of his business.

I'm working things out about Dair, now I've been here nearly a week. I know that his bark is worse than his bite, that he has nightmares that make him cry out in the night and that he has a child. I've watched him sleeping, seen him hold out his arms and whisper over and over, 'Ma little flower.' I also know better than to ask him about this. Questions make him sullen and silent. He disappeared for a whole day after I mentioned the tattoo of a rose on his arm. So I probably shouldn't say anything about the small white scar on his left temple.

'Do you want to hear something interesting?' Dair asks, his eyes gleaming.

'Yeah, if you stop flinching every time I cut,' I reply.

'I know where the new children's hospital is.'

I stop what I'm doing and look at him squarely in the mirror. 'How long have you known?'

He is counting on his fingers. I open and shut the scissor blades pointedly.

'Ten,' he says.

'Days, hours, minutes?' I press him.

'Months. And you shouldn't go there.'

'You knew I was looking for it. Why didn't you tell me before?' My voice has risen at least an octave.

'Lots of reasons. Because you'd have gone charging off there and you were in no fit condition,' Dair replies, equally loudly.

'It wasn't up to YOU!' I shriek, throwing down the scissors and storming off towards my house of books. I run inside and throw myself on my mattress. Dair has followed me and is standing outside my front door.

'OK, let's just say you could have evaded the security men with machine guns. Or mebbe navigated through the crowd outside, and climbed the wall in all the commotion of flying bottles and gas spray.' He is pacing up and down now, but not crossing my threshold. 'The virus is causing a lot of panic, Calypso. There aren't enough anti-viral drugs for everyone so people are fighting for them at the hospitals and distribution centres. It's getting ugly. And you wanted me to let you, in your sad state, get mixed up in that?'

'Yes. No. I don't know. You're nothing to do with me. Nobody. A crazy, hair-mad hobo who talks to a kid in his sleep. You don't know anything about me. And I'm not sad,' I spit.

Dair is staring at me, wounded. He looks ridiculous, with the right side of his hair shorter than the left.

'I know plenty about ye, as a matter o' fact. This isn't how it's supposed to be at all. I tell you the way it is. Then you should say, "OK, Dair, pal, agreed."

But no. You have to be lairy. I'm trying to look out for ye, and this is the thanks I get.'

My mouth starts to open in protest, but he is turning and walking away, out of Wonderland and down the stairs, three at a time.

I rush to one of the long windows and try in vain to force the catch back so I can open it and call out to him. It won't budge. A flash of blue tells me that Dair has already reached the overgrown gardens and done his vanishing act. Holy kumquats, that man is annoying!

But what if those things he said were true? How do I know he isn't just making it up?

See with your own eyes, Paper Clip. Yeah, Crease, I'll have to check it out myself. I need medical help. The goo from the aloe vera leaves Dair made into a poultice hasn't really stopped the pain. There's a bruise the size of Alaska right across my thigh and down my leg. It seems to be getting bigger, not smaller. I try not to look at it. I can't forget it, though. The pain is too intense.

I'm drawing a rose in the dust on the window pane,

wondering where Dair has sloped off to, hoping he's not too mad at me. It's the first time I've noticed the block of flats opposite and I realise its upper-floor windows look directly down into ours. I've got to hand it to Dair – he's vigilant about our privacy and the 'no candles or torches after dark' rule doesn't seem so completely lame now.

I'm not sure if it's the sun's reflection or my eyes straining through the dust, but I get the feeling that I am not the only one surveying this 'hood. A movement in the shadows behind the flats' glass and brick façade makes me blink. I rub the glass with my elbow and look again, more intently. Nothing. But the view is different. There was something there before that isn't there now. And the more I think about it the more I am sure it was a face. A face that was staring at me.

Chapter Eleven

I found a diary in a bin in the park this week, so now I can keep track of the day and date. Its last owner had torn out some pages before throwing it away. Apart from the ragged remains of the missing paper, it's in very nice condition. The front cover has some velvety swirls in black and pink and there's a ribbon to keep your place. The spine even has a pocket with a slim pen tucked inside.

I'm folding down the page corners each time I see the Face – there are four so far. It's there every evening, as the light fades. I can't see its expressions, but from its stillness I'm guessing it belongs to someone who is sad, or bored, or just plain nosy. It's a big head on a small body, which is another clue. So maybe it's a kid, a dwarf, or a life-size doll some joker is trying to scare me with.

I'm not frightened of it, though. In a strange way, I like it. It makes me feel less alone.

Whoever it is doesn't seem to want to get us evicted, but Dair and I have stopped using the front door just in case. Dair has smashed out some panes on the ground floor at the side of the building furthest from the street so we can climb in and out without being seen. He told me to stay inside my house and away from the windows too. The curfew on the streets has been extended and begins at eight o'clock at night now, so there are more patrols driving around the neighbourhood and he says I must be extra careful.

I've put blinds up so that there's no way I can be spotted from outside. One is actually made out of a woven cotton mat, wrapped round a piece of wood which is balanced between paperback copies of *Pride and Prejudice* and *Vampire Vacation*. I found them with about twenty other stories in a box in the hospital library at the end of this corridor. It was the only thing left in the room, apart from two wax crayons and a

beanbag with a big split in it. I mended the tear so now I have a chair of my own.

Most days, I curl into it like a banana, my feet sticking up at one end, and read to myself out loud, doing different voices for all the characters. I like feeling that there are lots of people around me.

'Can you tell the BBC to shut up, mate!' Dair often yells from next door. 'If I'd wanted a costume drama, I would have got a television.'

I don't think he minds, really. Sometimes, I know he comes and sits outside my house, just so he can listen. I try extra hard to read well then. I hear him laugh, or sigh, or tut tut, or draw his breath in, if it's an exciting bit. Once, he even corrected my pronunciation. Tee-to-taller seemed the oddest spelling I'd ever seen.

'I think you'll find it's "teetotaller",' a squeaky voice whispered through my window. 'It means someone who doesne drink a dram. Although I've never met such a person.'

I think Dair loves stories as much as I do. Maybe,

one day, he'll read me one of his favourites or, better still, make one up. It would be more fun than reading the horrible stories on the front pages of the papers about the rising violence on the streets since the food shops have stopped opening every day.

I don't want to think about that. I just focus on building my house, making it stronger and cosier. It even has a roof now, made from plastic sheeting, newspaper and pages from magazines, placed over a string frame. When I go to sleep, I'm staring up at wild horses galloping over the prairie, a double page spread from *National Geographic*. It's usually too dark to see them, unless there's moonlight. But in the morning they are always there to greet me – Flash and Racer, Sundancer and Wings.

I haven't tried to find the hospital. Every time I think about going, I feel too frightened by the things Dair said. Even going out foraging makes me very nervous. I do it at night, but before the curfew. The pain in my leg means I'm limping and can't run fast,

so getting caught is becoming more likely. Each time I jump into a skip to rummage for treasure, I wonder if a big net will be thrown over the top, trapping me, as the container is craned on to a low-loader and taken to the dump.

A homeless man was killed last week when the wheelie bin he was sleeping in was emptied into the crusher.

'Nowhere is safe now,' said Dair.

Nowhere except my house of books – and that's where I want to stay, with my little china Buddha and my dancing flower, my chandelier without a bulb and my framed photo of guinea pigs playing tug of war, until I can find the missing jigsaw pieces in my brain and put them back, one by one.

Dair and I haven't spoken much since our argument. He's keeping himself to himself. He hasn't sat in his chair for days and, apart from ear wigging at story time, he just stays in his space next door, making plans to storm the Hive and 'set the people free'. Sometimes, he

visits the library I've set up. He can borrow three books at a time for as long as he likes. But they must be ones from the shelf and not from my walls.

Andy the bear has a new job. He's my doorbell now, thanks to some new batteries I found in a paper bag at a bus stop. If I hear, 'I love you,' or, 'I just *lerve* honey,' I know I have a visitor. No surprises who it is.

I would give anything for it to be Little Bird. I want to speak to her so much, to hear her voice, to ask her a big 'Why?' Maybe I could call her? I'll need money to do that – some change or maybe a pound coin. I could find that tomorrow, if I look hard. But if I call her, the FISTS can find me – Dair says the pay machines are bugged.

I could write to her – but Dad thought our post was being opened before it got to us. If the FISTS are reading the mail, they would identify the postmark and the security teams would start scouring the area, inch by inch.

I've got to think this through, so I'm heading down

the stairs to the café, or what's left of it, where the smashed window pane has created our new entry and exit point. I used to sit in here with Mum during visiting time and there are still a few tables and chairs that escaped the clearance, and a sign saying *Have you washed your hands? Don't spread infection!* I haven't washed them, but I guess it doesn't matter now. The counter which used to have plates full of scones, cakes and biscuits is empty. There is no fat, smiley woman wearing a yellow apron by the till, and there are no kids with bandages or shaved heads or in wheelchairs waiting to be served.

I duck and climb through the gap in the window on to the flower bed next to the building. I walk down the path, rose thorns pricking at my arms and catching my sleeve on the way through.

The air is crisp and cool in the garden. It's the middle of the afternoon and already the light is beginning to fade. I sit on the bench and look at the low, grey clouds, with patches of blue in between. Little Bird and I used to play games with the sky. If you stare

up, after a while, your eyes adjust, and you can see patterns and shapes. There's an old man with a walking stick, a sheep with six legs, a palm tree – *waay!* – even a monkey!

And there's a woman, or a girl, with her face in her hands. Is she crying or screaming? The shape shifts and the clouds move on before I can decide.

I bring my knees up under my chin and wrap my arms round them. The vision was very unsettling and for some reason my heart is thumping and I'm afraid, almost too afraid to move. From not far away, maybe a mile or two, a familiar fairy song is floating towards me like the gulls on the breeze – *la la, la-la la.* I think of Mr Carter, the ice-cream man, and smile. I don't suppose he is selling many of those cones in this weather.

Moments later, a harsher noise – sirens, moving at speed – jars the peace. There's a single shot, like the explosion of a firework. Then silence.

My body is trembling. Images of Crease and Slee, lying face down on the pavement, hand-cuffed, flash

through my mind. I shake my head hard.

Don't do this, brain. That's not what I saw. But who knows what is happening on the other side of these walls?

Suddenly, there is a snap of a branch and I'm on my feet and my eyes are scanning this way, that way, and I'm ready to take off, because no one, no FIST, no Face, no teetotaller is going to take me to that centre where the sun doesn't shine.

'Grab the BLAGGER!' yells a deep voice and Dair comes crashing through the undergrowth, plastic mac flapping wide, arms forward like a sleepwalker, eyeballs almost popping out of his head, hair stiff with caked mud, one foot totally bare and bleeding.

'Aaargh!' I'm yelling, because he's yelling, but I don't know what I'm yelling about. And then I see it – a brown and white rabbit with a pink nose and floppy ears, hopping nimbly but with terrified eyes, backwards, forwards, sideways, in any direction to get away from Dair. It is holding up its front right paw and

I can see the flesh near the foot is red and raw.

'Dinner!' Dair shrieks as he rushes past me, and a backdraught of fruits of the forest follows. 'It's meat, mate, free-range, full-blooded, bona fide MEAT!'

'I thought you said you wouldn't eat meat because of the virus,' I call after him.

'Aye, well this bunny looks pretty healthy to me.' He crouches low in an attempt to corner the creature between the wall and the bench. 'In fact, it looks delicious and ma juices are rrrrrunning at the thought of sinking ma teeth into its . . .'

'It's injured and you're not killing it,' I say firmly, picking up the furry ball and cradling it in my arms.

'Finders keepers,' says Dair, getting closer.

'Losers weepers,' I counter, fixing him with my sternest stare. 'Bunny might have the virus – then what?'

'I die full up,' replies Dair with a shrug. His shoulders are heaving up and down. His neck is low, his cheeks sunken. He looks beaten, like a hyena that has lost its prey.

'It needs a sanctuary, just like us.' I stroke the animal's ears, holding it close.

'It's not living here, if that's what you're conniving,' states Dair, still getting his breath back. 'I'm asthmatic so there's to be no fur, no fur –' he wheezes – 'no further than the front door.'

'I can have a pet if I like. He can live in my house and he won't bother you.' I make my way back towards the café window. 'At least he'll be company, which is more than you are.'

I've realised two things in the last five minutes: that standing up for myself isn't so bad (if I don't do it, who will?) and that it's only the second time in my life I've been this honest with anyone, spontaneously, from the heart.

I glance back at Dair. He has his hands on his hips and looks like a pantomime pirate, his mouth open in a big 'O', his eyes wide and hurt.

'I hope it bites you, you evil-tongued harpy,' he retorts. 'Don't come running to me for sympathy when

your peepers stick together and your body writhes and shakes in agony on account of the poison from its putrid fangs.'

'I won't,' I reply.

Dair is lifting his arms up to the skies in a gesture of frustration and stamping his feet on the grass, like a spoiled kid. Then he stands still and says quietly, 'I wasn't really going to eat it. I couldn't. It's just that sometimes I . . .'

I'm not taking any notice. I'm already thinking about a name. I'm going to call this rabbit Furball.

Chapter Twelve

'You're going to like it here,' I'm telling Furball, who turns out to be a she, not a he. I'm stroking her soft stomach as she lies upside down in my arms. I'm hoping the cotton patch soaked in aloe vera and tied with ribbon round her bad foot will help it heal. Just holding her makes me happy. I don't remember the last time I felt like this.

'I wonder where you lived before,' I say to her. 'You don't look like a wild rabbit. You must have had an owner. Did something happen to you? Did you have to run away?' Her eyes watch me, unblinking and unreadable.

'You're safe now,' I whisper, hesitating to make it a promise, for those should never be trusted. The possibility that similar experiences have caused our

lives to collide makes me shiver. Perhaps this derelict hospital is really an ark, and more and more strays will come to take refuge from the hostile world outside. Maybe the old wards will fill up and the corridors will be full of children playing skittles and racing toy cars.

Maybe Dair, Furball and I are just the beginning?

'I've got a family too,' I explain. 'A mum and a dad. And a gran. But I had to run away from them too. Something bad happened – my brain won't tell me what it was – and I've come a long way and now I'm here. If you had looked at the kids in my class, you would never have picked me out as the one who would be living rough, hiding from the FISTS. I was always the mouse, squeaking quietly. I wonder what they're saying about me, the rest of 9B. Most of them won't believe I've gone. They think my life's sorted. Parents, house, happy family, no worries. But it takes more than a hutch and some hay to make a happy bunny, eh, Furball?

The rabbit is scratching her ear, sharp claws moving

so quickly I can barely see them. She is wriggling now, agitated. I put her down on my carpet and she hops to the front door. After sniffing the air around her, she scrabbles at the floor, as if digging a burrow, twitches her tail and promptly hops back inside again.

'Are you telling me this is your new home?' I ask. Then a thought occurs. 'I want to show you something, Furball. We're going to go and stand by the window, just for a minute. There's someone I want you to meet. Don't be scared. Here we are. I'm just going to hold you up – there's no need to scratch. You see that face over there? It's watching you, and watching me. I think it likes you. Yes, look, it's waving a hand. Hey, that's the first time it's tried to communicate.

'What do you think it means?'

Chapter Thirteen

Spiky tickles on my face, my chin, my hand. The brush of soft fur against my forehead. Small teeth pulling at the threads in my sleeve.

'Morning, Furball,' I say sleepily. When I open my eyes, her two pink ones are staring at me intently. 'What's up?'

Furball turns and hops out of my bedroom, heading towards the front door. I crawl off my mattress to see where she is scampering to and I'm surprised to find her balancing on her hind legs and scratching at the plyboard barrier with her front claws. I'm happy to see that her injured paw is mending nicely – that's good news after only five days.

'*Waay*, Flufty, what's the rush?' I glance back at my alarm clock shaped like a chicken – one of my

newest acquisitions. 'It's only eight o'clock.' Her scrabbling is getting more frenetic. 'OK, OK. I'm coming.'

It's a cold morning. I can see my breath rising like spirals of candy floss round a stick. I wrap the big travel rug from my bed round my shoulders, shove my feet into the bear slippers which are two sizes too big and pad to join Furball.

When I push the door open, she bunny hops at full speed across Wonderland to the corridor and then just looks at me, her ears flicking back and forth in a very agitated fashion. If she could speak, she would be saying, 'Come on!'

I follow her with a reluctant sigh, my bad leg causing me to suck my breath in as I feel a stab of pain. Furball is already heading off down the stairs. Bounce, bounce, bounce and she's at the bottom. As I shuffle after her, amused, thinking she is having a mad moment of rabbit rebellion, I soon see the reason for her strange behaviour. The shock of it makes me move

faster. I'm jumping three steps at a time, leaving my slippers behind.

'Dair! What are you doing?'

'What do you think I'm doing? Waiting for the number seven bus?' he answers quietly. He is lying on the floor of the old reception area, staring up at the domed ceiling. In the murky light of this winter morning, his face looks grey and his cheeks are as sunken as desert pools.

'Did you fall?' I ask, kneeling next to him.

'No, cherub, I thought I would jump from the top step to see if I could fly,' he answers with difficulty. He notices my look of increasing panic and decides to cut the sarcasm. 'I didna fall. I was going out to get us some supplies and my head was spinning like a big wheel so I lay down in this very salubrious spot and here we are.'

I peer into his eyes. 'You're a very strange colour.'

'That's good. If I looked well, I would be worried,' he says, trying to give me a little smile, which looks more like a grimace. I put my hand on his forehead.

The skin feels like ice. My fingers almost recoil.

'Cold?' he murmurs.

'As a box of frozen fish fingers,' I confirm. I'm thinking he would be much better off on my mattress, wrapped in blankets.

'I'll be fine.' It's as if he's reading my mind. 'Don't bother your wee self about me.'

'You can't lie here on this floor. I'll help you upstairs, come on.' I'm pulling at his arm, which is heavy and uncooperative. Slowly, Dair begins to respond and I take his weight as he attempts to stand. We sway from side to side, like a pair of drunkards.

'You're a good kid,' he tells me, attempting a wink.

With an arm round my shoulders and a hand on the wooden rail, Dair ascends the stairs, one at a time. He is trying to sing something about a stairway to heaven, which I hope isn't a bad sign. Furball is hopping behind us, her nose twitching.

I try to guide Dair towards my house, but he shakes his head and mutters, 'Ma chair, if you please,'

through chattering teeth. He is almost bent double now, his feet, in their mismatched trainers, scraping along the ground.

'There,' I say, relieved, as his large frame slumps down into the soft, blue cushions. I lay the rug over him and try to tuck it in, but his trembles have become more like convulsions and his arms are waving about erratically. I know what I have to do.

'I'm going to get help. You need an ambulance.'

'No,' he replies emphatically. 'It's no use, cherub. It's too late. I'm sorry.' His eyes are holding mine with a terrified gaze.

'Don't say that,' I argue with him, tears pricking behind my eyes.

'It's what happens when you don't do your job properly,' he says through chattering teeth.

'What job?' I ask.

'Looking after you.'

'We look after each other, that's the deal,' I say.

'Ye have to keep fighting them, Calypso, or they'll

take away everything that makes you who you are. Keep asking questions. Accept nothing you are told.' Dair is almost clawing at the scar on his left temple. 'Promise me you will.'

'What did they do to you?' I ask quietly.

'Put a microchip inside my brain. I was just a bairn. But they didna win. Nobody tells Dair McFarlane what to think. So c-c-cold,' he says, his body trembling.

'I'll get more blankets.' I run the few metres to my house and grab all the covers I can find. When I return to Dair, I see he has broken out in a sweat, even though he still feels freezing to the touch. I try to swaddle him in the extra layers, but he is thrashing about, trying to push them off. Furball is lying close to his feet, making a funny gurgling sound in her throat. I think it must be fear.

'Do you think you've got the virus?' I ask, bracing myself for Dair's reply.

'No. This is something much worse,' he whispers.

'You must take this, so you can get into the Hive and destroy it.' He is pressing the metal bottle top into my palm.

'Keep it safe until I get back.' I bend and am about to kiss Dair on the top of his head.

'Away wi' ye, ye blitherer,' he says, and he gives me a fleeting smile before closing his eyes.

There isn't a moment to lose. I rush to find my trainers and jacket and am still dressing as I descend the stairs again. Crawling through the hole in the café window will take too long, so I release the catch on the front door and open it, leaving it ajar for the medics I hope to persuade to come.

Never get caught.

Don't worry, Furball. I'll get Dair the help he needs. I'll watch them take him away and when it's safe, I'll come back here. I won't let them take me in. I won't.

As I set off down the moss-covered driveway at a painful sprint, there's a deep, terrible sensation in

my gut. It's like molten lava bubbling before it bursts through the top of a volcano.

There is an explosion coming. I can feel it with every beat of my heart.

Chapter Fourteen

Bam and *bam* the slam of feet on stone and throb of pain and questions in my brain – Why this? Why now? Look for help, for someone; kids on their way to school, a mum, a dad, a gran, a man in a van, a butcher, baker, candlestick maker, good knight with mobile, an angel with iPhone.

Stop. Breathe. Scan.

Thoughts are colliding in my brain, hot with friction, like an electric blade scything through wood. The streets are empty, apart from the rubbish the gulls are pulling from overflowing bins. Where is everyone?

It's an offence to knock on a stranger's door, but it's a crime to let a friend die, so in less than a minute I am at a house at the top of the hill, and the door is opening, almost before my finger has pressed the bell.

'I need an ambulance for someone who is ill,' I explain. 'Can you help me, please?'

A woman of about sixty, with white hair and a sharp face, is staring at me through thick glasses. She looks curious, but irritated, like a suspicious old person who hates the world.

'I'm sorry to ask, but it's an emergency,' I continue.

The woman raises her eyebrows, sighs and closes the door.

'No!' I yell, banging on it as hard as I can. 'Don't ignore me. I just need you to make one call.'

There is no response from inside.

Little Bird would never have turned away a child, not even one dressed as raggedly as me. But laws are laws, as Dair keeps saying, and people are afraid.

A church bell sounds somewhere in town. Eight thirty and still no thrum of traffic, no buses bursting with kids and office workers, no hygiene trucks, clearing up the dead animals after last night's street cleansing.

I haven't checked my diary for a while and it's

dawning on me that today must be Sunday. This place may be having a lie-in, but I have to find help urgently. I will ask the first person I see. Too bad that it's a paper boy of about my age, who suddenly hurtles past on a bike, talking into a mobile, balanced between his shoulder and his left ear.

'Hey!' I shout. 'Can I borrow your phone?' But he is already a dot at the bottom of the hill.

I'm running as fast as my legs can carry me, hoping I might be able to catch up with him on his rounds, but as I near the end of the steep slope I have lost sight of him and his bike.

'What you runnin' for?' asks a small girl with strawberry-blonde ringlets under a pink wool hat. She is playing with a doll's pram in a front garden next to where I am bent double, trying to get my breath back.

'I wanted to borrow a phone from the paper boy,' I tell her. This sounds really stupid.

'You can use mine,' she says. 'If you give me a sweetie.'

'I don't have any sweeties, but I'll get you some — whatever you want,' I say, trying to keep the desperation out of my voice.

'I want lemon fizzes,' the girl announces.

'Then I'll go to the sweet shop, after I've used your phone,' I say, smiling.

'Promise?' she asks, looking very earnest.

'Promise,' I agree. I'm not letting myself worry about how I would pay for them.

'Here y'are, then,' she says, rummaging under the covers in her pram and producing a plastic handset. 'You press the numbers on the front and guess who answers?' she asks darkly.

'Who?' I respond, crushed.

'Barbie,' she confides, in hushed tones.

'I need a real phone. I'm sorry.' I feel totally despondent. 'Do you have one inside your house?'

'Course I have,' she tells me, tidying her pram covers.

'Would it be OK if I come in and use it? I need to call the hospital.' Irritation is creeping into my voice.

The girl looks at me for a moment and smiles. 'You are funny,' she says. 'But you're not allowed inside. Can I still have my sweeties?'

'Can you get your mum or dad, please?' I request, trying to stay calm.

'No,' she answers sadly, and something in her voice prevents me from pressing her further. There must have been a family tragedy here – maybe her parents died from the virus. I feel sorry and full of panic all at the same time.

'Will you get my lemon fizzes now?' she asks, softly, her blue eyes round with hopefulness. Any other time, I would say yes. Any other time, I would get her more bags than she has ever dreamed of.

'Gotta go,' I say, and give her a little wave. Her small hand waves back. The other one is wiping tiny tears from her eyes.

I'm jogging with a heavy heart, weighing up my options. There is an answer to my problem. If I find the hospital, I can get an ambulance for Dair myself.

And maybe I can also find the friendly doctor and get some help for my thigh. If it comes out that I've been near Dair, I will be quarantined, so I must be careful what I say.

More than anything, I want to speak to Little Bird, to hear her say she loves me. Something in my encounter with the small girl has left me with a deep, scary fear that I may never see my mother again.

Suddenly, an image of her face flashes through my mind. She is mouthing something at me. There is no sound, just the shape of the word, repeated many times. I struggle to lip-read. Is this my imagination playing tricks or is it a real memory? 'Ra, ra, ra,' she seems to be shouting, yet her tongue moves to the roof of her mouth each time.

Caly, you idiot, it's obvious what she's saying. She is telling you to run.

My throat has tightened. I can't breathe. I have to stand very still. I lean against the wall outside a newsagents, which is closed. There is a sign on the

door that reads: 'Due to illness, this shop will be shut until further notice.' I see the phrase but it has no meaning. A large piece of my puzzle has just fallen into place and the shock of it has caused my knees to give way.

Little Bird was trying to protect me – from what; from whom?

Nine dongs of the bell. The tolling is morphing into the noise of sirens, which are approaching at speed from the direction of the town centre. I'm trembling at the thought that someone has reported me, and I start to move towards the cover of a deep doorway. Just moments later, a fire engine thunders past me up the hill, followed by a police patrol car with its warning lights flashing.

None of the passengers look at me as they pass. All the same, I try to conceal the expression of complete terror which must be etched on my face. Idiot, Caly. These guys might be the short cut to the help Dair

needs. Tell them what's happened, then disappear.

I'm attempting to jog back up the hill, my good leg taking most of the strain. I don't remember it being this far – but memory isn't my strong point. I'm rehearsing what I will say to the emergency team when I find them: 'There's a man who is very ill on the first floor of the old hospital.' That has all the information, without implicating me, I hope.

But what do I do if they ask me to show them where?

Say you heard him shouting from the window. Say anything to stay out of their grasp.

Focus on getting up this pig of a hill. I've decided the local residents must have legs like mountaineers. Maybe they are all artists too, as the houses are painted pastel shades of blue, green, lilac and pink. Looking at them is like watching a picture book unfolding.

I don't like the way the story is going, though. A large crowd has gathered in the street and is blocking my path. Plumes of black smoke are rising into the

clear blue sky from behind the terraced houses at the top of the incline. It must be a huge fire and all these people have been evacuated from their homes.

But as I battle my way through the groups of bystanders, I begin to realise that the smoke has a much more terrifying source.

The hospital is alight, orange and yellow flames poking through the top floor windows like serpents' tongues. The fire engine is parked in the grounds, near the bench where I found Andy. Fire fighters are standing on a platform, directing large hoses through the windows. All the glass panes are missing, probably blown out by the ferocity of the heat inside.

There is a lot of commotion. The police have cordoned off the area in front of the danger site and are telling the crowd to 'Keep back, for your own safety,' through loudhailers.

'DAIR! FURBALL!' I'm yelling, trying to push my way through the mass of bodies, some in dressing gowns and pyjamas, clutching mugs of hot liquid,

jostling for the best view. I'm hoping with every fibre of my being that my furry friend has followed her animal instincts and hopped away to safety.

No one is being allowed through the barrier, but, being what my dad calls a 'short arse', I manage to duck under it and I'm running to the first person in uniform I can find. It's a motorbike cop, who is speaking into a microphone on his crash helmet. I grab his arm to get his attention.

'There's a sick man in there. You've got to help him. Please,' I'm begging.

The cop looks at me, frowns and dismisses me with a flick of his wrist, as if I'm a fly that has settled on his skin. He is walking away, still speaking into his headset, joining colleagues who are moving the tape to allow another fire engine through.

'Will someone listen to me? There's a sick man on the first floor!' I scream, but the vehicle's siren and the noise of the crowd are drowning me out. I shout until my voice goes hoarse. There's nothing for it –

I'll have to take matters into my own hands and force them to follow me in.

As I begin to run towards the burning building, I feel the intensity of the flames and start to choke on the smoky fumes pouring from inside. Any moment now, I expect a fire fighter to lunge at me and try to stop me gaining entry. Instead, I am almost crushed by several men in protective gear, running out of the building.

'Get back!' they warn and two seconds later there is a massive *CRACK* and the sound of splintering wood and bending metal and, suddenly, the whole roof falls in, in slow motion, sending clouds of debris in all directions.

The crowd falls silent. Everyone stands still. Then there is coughing and hushed murmurs of surprise. When the dust settles, the blackened top floor is completely exposed, like a giant doll's house. Only the shell of the walls and windows remain. Parts of the floor are also gone. If I ever get back inside my house, I will be looking straight at the stars.

Acrid fumes of charcoal and wet wood hang in the air. The dramatic collapse has put out the fire, so the water hoses are being reeled in. A policeman is confirming that there are no casualties on the ground (what about inside?) but he asks for an ambulance in case anyone is suffering from smoke inhalation.

I don't understand any of this. My head is hurting trying to make sense of it. There was nothing flammable on the second floor – just empty rooms and floor boards. There was no electricity or gas to ignite a blaze.

I don't believe Dair would have started this fire. He was just sitting in his chair – too ill to move. Surely they would have seen him when they swept through each floor and brought him out! I can't think about the other possibility: that he was still there when the roof fell in. That I've let him down so terribly and I will never set eyes on him again.

'Yeah, it could be arson,' the policeman in charge is saying into his radio. 'There were reports of a hobo living rough here and evidence of personal belongings

found on the first floor. Get this – it was all kept in a house made of books. Clearly a nutter. No sign of him before the roof went, no body remains, although he could have been hiding somewhere. We'll do a final sweep through to secure it, then get the place boarded up. Sooner it's demolished the better.'

The hospital is steaming gently in the winter morning sun. Has my house been destroyed too? Did the strength of a thousand paperbacks, two Bibles, a Koran, *The Tibetan Book of the Dead*, a fishing encyclopaedia and *The Complete Works of Shakespeare* withstand the onslaught? Did those big-booted feet of the emergency team kick their way through my rooms?

Have I lost my world for a second time – and the only friends I had in it?

As the crowd begins to disperse, I notice something glinting on the ground and stoop to pick it up.

'Finders keepers,' says a voice close to me – honest to God, it's Dair's, I would swear to it – but when I

turn round all I see are the backs of strangers, moving away slowly.

Clutched in the palm of my hand is a metal bottle top. It looks just like Dair's special one. 'Promise me you'll keep fighting them,' he said. I couldn't promise, not just because of a metal disc. *Sorry, Dair. It's not a key to the Hive. It's just a bit of junk. But I'll keep it, because I know you want me to. Maybe they were still out to get you, just like you thought. Each time I hold the disc, it will remind me to stay strong and watch my back.*

I tuck it deep into my trackie pocket.

No body remains. The words resonate in my mind, a chilling reminder that Dair is missing and that I must pull myself together if I want to survive. I'm at crisis point and there is only one person who can help me; the same person I must warn before it's too late.

Chapter Fifteen

I'm at the checkpoint where all vehicles are scanned before entering, or leaving, the zone. It took nearly two hours to make it this far. My thigh is throbbing and I feel weak with cold, despite the old jacket I found in a skip after setting off. I was going to try to go across country, but it will soon be curfew time, and I can't risk being seen leaving the controlled area.

The darkness is protecting me. I'm hiding at the back of a toilet block. From here, I can see all the cars and lorries in the queue. One by one, they are being swept by a scan gun. Then the automatic barrier lifts and they drive away.

Crouch low. Breathe. Make a plan.

I've decided to stow away in the back of an open truck. I need to choose carefully. It mustn't have sides

that are too high. I'll need to cat leap in once it has passed through the barrier. It will be moving, so I'll have to use all my free-running skills to keep pace with it and make the leap. My heart is banging in my chest, reminding me that time is ticking away. What if there isn't a suitable vehicle? My spirit sinks at the thought of a journey overland, through the night.

I look at the queue of cars stretching back into the darkness. There are two lanes of them and the *thrum* of their engines sounds like a swarm of bees moving closer, very slowly. About fifty metres away, there are raised headlights. As they approach, I see they belong to a large black van with an open back, and scaffolding poles tied down inside.

This is the one. There's nothing else in the line that I can get into. It's now or never. I try to steady my breathing, which has become shallow and panicky. I watch the van intently as it moves forward and stops on the scanning grid. There are two people in the cab: a stocky male driver and a younger man with spiky hair.

A blue light sweeps over the vehicle. There is a high-pitched *beep beep* noise and the barrier begins to rise.

Bam and *bam*, my feet are slamming on the ground. Head down and push and push and *whoooah*, the rush of air against my face! Speed up and force my legs to sprint, so fast they are a blur of motion. Three, two, one and LEAP and land and grip the side and flip and tip and curl and roll and holy mangoes. Made it!

I'm on all fours, crouched between scaffold poles and the side of the van, ribs rising and falling heavily. I'm so full of adrenaline I can't feel any pain in my bad leg. The poles are a great camouflage. I slide underneath them. I mustn't relax. I need to be ready to jump out once we reach the barrier at the end of the motorway, the entrance to my home zone.

It's a bumpy, noisy ride. The van is travelling fast, making the poles rattle and clank together. I'm estimating that the journey will take about half an hour. It's hard to gauge the passing of time. There is nothing to do but stare at stars.

I'm almost lulled into sleep by the motion so I make myself try to join the dots in the sky. One giant spider's web later and we seem to be slowing down. Darkness is replaced by bright light – we must be approaching the next control point.

Time to skedaddle. I'm peering over the side of the van, waiting for my moment. The vehicle slows to a crawl. I take a deep breath and vault as silently and lightly as possible, landing on the tarmac. As soon as my feet touch the ground, I am off, like a bat flitting away from the dawn. I'm hiding in the bushes at the side of the road before you can say *mai pen rai*.

I know the direction to take. I can see the Social Observation Tower in the distance, lit up like a skinny needle. My house is east of here. I'll follow the main road towards town, staying out of sight behind the grass banks, and cross when the traffic thins to a trickle.

I'm running on autopilot. Seconds, minutes, hours. I have no idea how long I've been pounding across wet soil, grass, tarmac and pavements. I only

know one thing. My feet are taking me home.

There is no one about by the time I reach the trading estate. I follow the road as it weaves between warehouses. Very soon, I am jogging up the alley which leads to our back gate. It is locked. I vault the fence and stay crouched amongst the plants by our shed. There are lights on downstairs. The curtains are drawn in the lounge but the kitchen blind isn't down, so I can see it in detail. It all looks so familiar. There is even a trace of lemon grass on the night breeze. I want to walk in the back door like nothing has happened, hold my mother so tight and hear her say she loves me.

But I can't go in. The FISTS might have set up listening devices. I must watch and wait and hope that my mum is here, that she comes outside. She's the reason I've risked coming home. I need her to tell me everything is going to be all right. But that might be impossible. I have to warn her that she's in danger. She's the mother of a free runner, an enemy of the System.

My dad will just be white hot angry with me for causing trouble, but Mum's the one who worries about me. She'll understand that I've blanked out the events of that night and she'll tell me what happened.

Khoon phra chuay! Little Bird has appeared at the kitchen window. She is looking out, her face drawn and tired. She is even smaller than I remember and sadder than I could ever have imagined. I'm shaking like a jelly, not sure what to do. Why am I afraid to approach the person I love most in the world?

The back door is opening and my mum is stepping out, her arms folded against the cold night air. She is peering towards the bushes where I'm hiding and muttering to herself, taking a deep breath, shaking her head.

'My *kon dee* . . .' she says softly.

I nearly melt when I hear her special Thai name for me. I am about to jump up and run to her when I see a policewoman standing in the kitchen doorway. I want to yell at my mum to get out of there, but no sound

comes. Little Bird turns and moves inside, closing the door. I see her putting the kettle on. This might be my last chance.

I creep across the lawn and stay low under the kitchen window. I can hear voices – my mum's and the woman's. They are speaking quietly. Little Bird doesn't seem frightened by her. I wonder where my dad is. At the pub, probably. I don't understand why there's a cop in our house and why my mum is making her tea. Maybe she's waiting for me and Mum is just playing along. If she's under house arrest, what choice does she have?

I wait until the talking stops and raise my head a fraction above the window sill. Little Bird is taking milk from the fridge. She glances my way and drops the carton. Its contents spill on the floor.

'I love you,' I mouth at her. She moves to the door swiftly and opens it. She is crying and speaking. I can just make out what she is saying.

'Take care of my child, St Francis.'

'Mum!' I whisper loudly. But the door has closed again and I can see the shadow of the cop moving about. The sink tap is turned on. I should use the noise as cover and make for the bushes. But I feel paralysed, as if I've turned to stone.

Did Little Bird see me? If she did, why didn't she speak directly to me? And what was all that about St Francis? Mum's a Buddhist, not into saints. Maybe she's trying to tell me it's not safe. How can it be, with a policewoman in the house? She's protecting me, just like she has, every day of my life.

It's dangerous to stay. It's dangerous to go. The sit-u-a-shun is bad, every which way. I think I'm in shock. My thoughts are jumbled, full of voices, shouting. I put my hands over my ears. It doesn't help. The yelling gets louder and my thigh starts to ache so badly I feel sick.

I have to get myself to a safe place, somewhere I can get my head down, think things through. And there's only one destination that ticks that box.

Chapter Sixteen

Om mani padme hum. *Bless you, Little Bird. Bless me.* Na myoho renge kyo. *May everything be as it should. May there be peace. May our worries be lifted. May our hearts be full of joy. May Dair and Furball be safe, wherever they are tonight.*

I'm climbing into the hospital through the hole in the café window, the one place that seems not to have been boarded up. Dawn is breaking, but all I want to do is lie down and sleep. I've been running for hours across fields and through woods. There was no Mr Carter, no black van, to give me a lift this time. I had to use my free-running skills to stay off the roads. Every part of me feels bruised and battered. I can't put my full weight on my left leg either.

It's a miracle I've made it back.

I am grateful I've not been caught. I am grateful I

have clothes to wear, unlike some kids. I am grateful for shelter in this building. I am trying to remember all the things to be grateful for, so that I don't turn into a crazy person.

'My *kon dee*.' That's what she said, my poor mother. She looked so sad, her arms wrapped round her small body. Was Dad there in the background, ready to come down on me like a ton of bricks for the shame I've brought on the family? Has he been twisting her arm, the way he sometimes does, when she doesn't give him full attention? Has he shopped me to the authorities? Is that why there was a policewoman in the house, waiting?

I have slunk back here like a guilty cat. I had to wait until first light to enter the grounds. There were FISTS and police swarming all over the place. Then the men in white vans arrived to secure the doors and windows. Lucky for me they weren't too thorough.

Back inside, where Dair lay, there are only sodden tiles covered in a layer of thick slime. My feet skid and

slide. The muted light of morning is disorientating. I reach for the wooden rail, which is no longer there.

The steps are slippery too. I place my trainers sideways and climb like a scuttling crab on shifting sand. I reach the landing. There are wide holes where the ceiling has become sky. The corridor is now an assault course of masonry and massive metal lintels, some upended like megaliths. It's as if someone has dropped Stonehenge from a great height.

The name above the ward entrance has lost more letters. It just reads *Wonder* now. Maybe that is all we are left with, when our world crumbles. Unanswered questions and awe.

I'm staring into the space ahead. It's the same place I left yesterday, but it looks as if it's had the opposite of a digital make-over. Its muted colours have faded to black. Soot coats the walls, window panes and Dair's precious chair, which is in its familiar position, but minus its blankets.

I force myself to look at the strange, dark silhouette

to my right. It reminds me of the woodland cottage in Snow White: ramshackle, with crooked lines. By some miracle, most of my house seems to be standing. I move towards it like a soldier walking through a minefield. The floorboards could give way any minute. If I fall, no one will hear me cry out.

The front door has disappeared, along with the library. The plastic sheet on the roof has spared the interior the worst of the falling debris, but smoke has penetrated everywhere. All the books have black covers and edges and there is dust a couple of centimetres thick on all the flat surfaces.

My kitchen drawer has been upturned, its contents strewn across the cotton rug. With a sinking feeling in the pit of my stomach, I realise my lighter is missing.

I locate my torch and in the glare of its white beam, conduct a more thorough search. This reveals many things I would rather not have discovered: that my clothes store has gone from its box and my curtains have been wrenched from their fragile tracks. My

wooden photo frames and both my pillows have been spirited away too.

But sitting sadly on the bare mattress, there is a small, black bear with glass eyes downcast.

'Andy!' I exclaim, a nanosecond of joy quickly dulled by the realisation that someone must have put him there, the same someone who has taken most of my flammable possessions, carried them up to the top floor, stacked them on top of each other and set light to them.

I'm curling up on my damp, dirty mattress, Andy held tight in my arms, my body shuddering under the weight of this awful truth. The worst part is I won't ever know why Dair did this. Some deep instinct is telling me he is far away and I will never see him again.

I thought we were friends. I thought we looked out for each other. Just like I believed our life at the hospital could stay a secret and that seeing my mum would make everything better. As usual, I was wrong about everything.

I am too exhausted to get undressed. My bad leg now feels like it is being burned at the stake. I lie on my mattress and hope the oblivion of sleep will come quickly. My eyelashes are heavy with salty liquid, but I'm too tired to cry. My brain is throbbing with a regular, insistent beat. Maybe it's an echo of my heart, letting me know it's still working, despite being broken. Maybe it's just a headache, although it feels more like the stomp of a marching army.

What good are memories if they are so painful? The night before last, Furball was sleeping next to me, her cute whiskers twitching every time she breathed out. I miss the warmth of her small body, the smell of her fur. Three of us felt like a family. I don't think I want to stay here on my own. I hope, when I close my eyes, that this damaged, desecrated den will swallow me up for good and that wherever Dair has gone I can follow him, if only in my dreams.

'Not exactly the coolest crib on the planet, is it?' says a husky voice, very near by. I open my eyes, try to

scramble to my feet and scream, all at the same time. The wall of books between the bedroom and kitchen gives way and as I sprawl across a hundred volumes of bedtime stories *Grimm's Fairy Tales* lands on my head with a heavy thump.

Chapter Seventeen

'Who are you?' I bark. The looming shape isn't clear in the dim morning light. I fumble for my torch. When I click it on, its beam illuminates the face of a boy, blinking at me and smiling. It's a familiar shape, one that is framed by a huge mass of thick, curly brown hair.

'I'm Alfie. I live over there,' he replies, motioning with a small hand. 'I'm the one who waved at you and your rabbit.'

'You're the FACE,' I exclaim, surprise causing me to make a strange horror-movie-type noise in my throat.

'Not that scary, I hope.' He does a Frankenstein impression then morphs into a sweet choirboy, to prove his point. 'Anyway. I thought you might want some company.'

My head is still hammering and it's hard to think

clearly. I haul myself to my feet. I notice we are about the same height, but Alfie is wider than me all over.

'How did you get in?' I ask, suspicious that this might be a trap to lure me into the child detention van.

'Same way as you, through the café window,' he replies. 'It's well cool that they didn't board it up. Saw the fire. Man! All that smoke . . . Are you OK?' he asks gently.

'I wasn't here. I mean, it started after I —' It's difficult to talk about the events of yesterday. I'm still so confused, not sure if this is a waking dream. 'Shouldn't you be getting ready for school or something?'

'Yeah. Can't stay long. Anyway, my mum will be back from work soon, so I'd better get going.'

'She leaves you alone at night?' I say, surprised.

'It was the only job she could get, monitoring the CCTV cameras in the town centre.' He shrugs. 'She hates it, but we need the money.' He thrusts his hands into the pockets of his low-slung jeans and glances at the floor. I notice that both his trainer laces are undone.

'Don't you get scared?' I ask.

'Only when I look in the mirror,' he answers, his wide smile and thick eyebrows stretching into the funniest contortions. One moment, he looks like a geeky scientist, the next a naughty puppy with droopy ears. I start to laugh and Alfie gives me a big grin. 'What about you?'

I want to say, 'I'm afraid every minute of every day,' but that sounds lame so I raise my shoulders in a 'maybe' sort of gesture.

'Do you know where the crazy guy has gone?' asks Alfie. The huskiness has returned to his voice. Must be the damp air in here.

'Nope. And Dair's OK,' I state defensively. 'I've lost Furball,' I add sadly. 'I'm going to search for her in the grounds tomorrow, just in case she's hiding.'

'Good plan.' Alfie nods. There's an awkward silence.

'Don't you want to know what I'm doing here?' I ask him warily.

'Living a life of wild adventure?'

'Don't be silly. I'm only thirteen.'

'We could be twins. Kicking!' says Alfie, pleased.

'Get lost, I'm half Thai.' I realise how nice it is to have someone to talk to again.

'Have you ridden an elephant?' he asks, impressed.

Only in my dreams, Little Bird. 'Nope,' I admit. 'Not many of those in Collingford.'

'That's in Zone Four, isn't it?' Alfie asks, then notices my discomfort. 'Look, you don't have to explain if you don't want to.'

I hold his gaze for a moment, wondering if I dare begin. Can I trust him? He's watched me for three weeks and hasn't reported me, not even to his mum. It would be so great to have a mate my age to share secrets with. But it feels too soon, too risky, to open up.

'I get it. Mystery Girl,' he says. 'That's what I've called you on my blog.'

I look horrified at this and am about to lay into him about the danger of meddling in other people's lives, when he puts a finger to his lips. 'Kidding,' he says

quietly. 'Blogs have been banned, anyway.'

'Since when?' I ask.

'A few weeks ago. Some new law from Europe. The president said it was a good idea,' he replies. 'Mum calls him Banana Head.'

'So you haven't written anything about me, or told anyone about me – not your best friend, your worst enemy, your auntie, your cousin, your newspaper boy?' I press him, agitated.

'Look, I just wanted to see if you were all right.' He seems offended and is half turning, as if he is about to leave.

'I'm sooty and tired and confused, but good, thanks,' I tell him, holding out my hand.

'Well, Sooty, it was nice to meet you.' Alfie takes my hand and shakes it. His touch is so gentle I can hardly feel it.

'You can visit me again, if you like,' I say, as warmly as I can.

'If I'm not too booked up.' He's smiling now,

pointing at my paperbacks. 'And if the place hasn't fallen down. Might be a good idea to live downstairs,' he suggests.

'So you'll come?'

'Yabradoodle,' he barks.

'Promise?' I press him.

'On my fart and hope to fly,' he answers, hand on his heart.

'Are you always this mad?' I ask.

Alfie grins and starts to move away.

'My name's Calypso, if you want to know.'

He takes this in, frowns, then shakes his head.

'Sooty's better,' he replies, giving me a little wave. Moments later, he is gone. When I glance at my clock, it reads seven a.m.

Chapter Eighteen

I'm moving house – downsizing. I decided I should take Alfie's advice. It's probably not safe to live on the first floor any more. He's here helping me carry my stuff down to the café. He kept his promise.

'Can't you live in a sleeping bag like any normal runaway, Sooty?' he asks, puffing under the weight of a big box of books. He's the complete opposite of Crease, I'm thinking. Under that baggy Superman T-shirt, he's probably just jelly.

'I like having walls,' I reply, following him down the stairs with a long column of novels between my hands. 'And I don't like nicknames, OK? You can call me Caly or Calypso. Not Paper Clip, not Miss Saigon and definitely not Sooty.'

Alfie is looking at me, quite perplexed. 'Yes, Your

Highness.' He's resting his box on the wooden rail and letting it slide down to the point where the wood disappears.

After looking everywhere for Furball, without success, I've spent hours washing soot and grime from my things. Many of the books were beyond hope, but there are enough left to make a good-sized room. It will be a studio flat, rather than a bungalow, but I can always extend once I get my supplies up again.

Tea-light candles rescued from a skip are illuminating our path. The stairs have dried out and are no longer slippery. We've done at least twenty trips up and down already and my leg is being a pain. So is Alfie.

'Nelly,' he chortles, from the bottom of the steps, pointing out that my shadow resembles a two-legged elephant with a trunk.

'Belly,' I retort. Alfie wobbles his stomach obligingly, does a weird little pharaoh dance, then picks up his box and loafs off towards the café.

It's like we've known each other a long time, yet

it's only been a day. I've never met anyone so easy to be with. He's really kind and funny. When I laugh, the horrible mesh of tangled wires in my head feels like it's starting to unravel. Maybe the answers to my three big puzzles – my memory blank, the mystery of Dair's disappearance and, now, Mum's weird behaviour – will magically reveal themselves, like stars when the clouds pass.

I bet Alfie's got loads of friends, especially girls. He really listens to what I'm saying and he doesn't try to make me feel small, like other boys do. Like my dad does. Alfie knows loads of things about the world, sensible things, but he isn't always showing off. He could use a few tips about hair care, though. I don't think his crazy mop has ever seen a brush, let alone any conditioner.

I suddenly stop in my tracks. There is something I need to check out. Something so obvious, I should have thought of it straight away. I drop my books and return to the first floor, scrabbling over debris to get to

Dair's bathroom. Lined up neatly on a shelf under the blackened mirror are ten different shampoos, all grimy with smoke deposits. There are also several containers of gel, treatments for split ends and henna oil for healthy gloss. He didn't take them with him. So maybe he's going to come back?

'Don't be too hopeful,' Alfie cautions, when I tell him this hot piece of news in the café.

'You don't understand,' I explain. 'He was obsessed with his hair. He wouldn't have gone without them, not for good.'

'There's no telling with crazy people.' Alfie shrugs. He's rubbing his eyes and blinking like a Thai bear-cat in headlights.

'What happened to your X-ray vision?' I ask, with mock seriousness.

'Who said that?' he answers with a grin, looking left and right.

I get the feeling he doesn't want to talk about Dair. He's pacing up and down now with a very silly walk.

'What are you doing?'

'Measuring up, so your walls are the same length.' He looks like a chicken. I can't help giggling. 'You won't think it's funny when you get subsidence,' he warns, waggling his finger at me. He reminds me of Mr Pepper, the security officer on our estate, who checks us in and out of the gates and whose face starts to twitch if he has to alter the computer entry more than twice an hour. 'Don't push your luck,' he says to all the kids, in exactly the same tone.

'I'd like it to be sunny,' I tell Alfie. 'The door should be here and the window there, so I look out over the garden.'

'And what sort of style would Madam like her crib? Georgian, with pillars; Gothic, with gargoyles; eco, with grass on top?' he asks, pretending to make notes.

'I'd like it to be tall and preferably made of gingerbread.'

Alfie nods and scribbles on his imaginary pad. 'And will that be a cherry on the top?' he says.

'Definitely.'

'It might have to be a flower. I'm clean out of cherries.' Alfie has found my plastic sunflower, which is still grimy with soot. He stretches and holds it above his head, indicating where the roof of my new house will be.

'Perfect,' I say, clapping with excitement.

'Don't speak too soon. I've never made a house before,' warns Alfie.

'Yeah, but Superman can do anything.'

Even in the dimly lit darkness, I can tell that Alfie is blushing.

Chapter Nineteen

Cold night air in my hair, eyes streaming winter tears, nose like an ice cube, mouth a big 'O', cheeks numb, arms outstretched, gloved hands gripping hard, body arched, foot flapping, scarf-muffled shriek of perfect pandemonium – we're FLYING!

'ALFIE!' I'm yelling.

'Whoaooh!' comes the reply, from behind.

We've chosen our moment, waited until the road was clear, and now we're careering to the bottom of the hill, weaving from tarmac to pavement, dodging the bumps and cracks, the potholes, rubbish cartons and parked cars. We're travelling so fast everything around us is a blur. We're superheroes on silver speed machines: invincible, unstoppable.

Two silver scooters. Two kids with a mission.

Two perfect minutes. Maybe good things always come in twos.

'Sooty,' Superman is calling. 'My brakes don't work!'

Alfie is zooming past me, a look of terror and delight on his flushed face. His cheeks are vibrating with the speed. His left foot is pressing down on the metal bar which is supposed to lock the back wheel, but nothing is happening, or so he wants me to think.

Up ahead, the road curves and levels out by a green. Both of us begin to slow and we roll to a halt next to a covered bus stop opposite the beach.

'*Jaaeo!*' I declare. 'This is soooooo cool!'

'Yabradabradoodle,' agrees Alfie.

We are not alone. There is an old woman sitting on the wooden bench, waiting for a bus. She is staring with wide eyes at our scooters. Her eyes are moving on to me – not surprising as I must look a real sight in Alfie's mum's old pink raincoat and purple scarf-and-gloves combo. It's not a good idea for us to hang about and I motion to Alfie that we should skedaddle, but there

is mischief in his eyes and he sounds the horn on his handlebars.

'Holy Mother of God,' the woman murmurs, crossing herself, before getting up and shuffling away. She glances back at us every so often and crosses herself again. Our adrenaline spills over into laughter and we sprawl across the seat, clutching our bellies.

'What was that all about?' I ask, between outbursts of snorting.

'Banana head,' Alfie replies, making loopy signs with his hand.

I'm sorry she was scared by the sight of two dishevelled kids on scooters. Maybe her eyesight was bad and we looked like aliens on silver skis. It's about seven p.m., an hour before curfew, and people get jumpy.

It's been the best night for treasure. We've been hunting for books. Books for walls, books for tables, books for a bed frame. We've found fifty already, most of them in the paper skip at the town's official dump. It's easy to squeeze on to the site through a gap in

the corrugated metal warehouse. We go there at night when it's closed to the public. That way, we only need to avoid the security guards.

We found the scooters there, right on top of the metal bin. It was the first time I've seen Alfie nearly cry.

'Always wanted one of these,' he said. 'That's yabrakickingdoodle,' he added, once we were far enough away and could try them out.

Checking out charity shop doorways was a piece of cake on two wheels. We whizzed round, filling our carrier bags with any books we could find amongst the piles of donated items left after closing time. We hung our wares from the handlebars and moved on to roadside skips, which added a backpack and a kite to our haul. Alfie wanted me to take a blue Perspex loo seat with shells in it too, but I told him we only ever take what we need. That's the rule. Although, on second thoughts, it would have made my bathroom look ten times nicer.

I had such a good time I'd even forgotten about home and Dair and Furball for a while. And another really great thing – my leg isn't hurting nearly so much. The horrible pain is more of an ache now. That's another reason to celebrate.

'Let's play skidders,' suggests Alfie, suddenly jumping to his feet and pulling me up by my arm.

'No idea what that is,' I say.

'Don't tell me you've never skimmed stones across the water, Sooty,' he sighs.

'We don't come to the seaside much. My dad doesn't like it.' I have a mental image of my father throwing down his bag of chips in disgust after a seagull pooped on his shirt several summers ago.

'It's easy peasy scratch my fleazy,' says Alfie. 'Come on.'

We're crossing the wide road, scooters in hand, and running over the grass that gives way to a tarmac promenade before I can say nobradoodle. We are racing down narrow steps on to the shingle, which is

bathed in deep lilac light from the half moon hiding behind purple clouds.

We stand on a ridge of stones and look out across the inky blackness rising and subsiding with a great *harrumph*, like an old dinosaur dragging its weight and sputtering spumes of white foam at our feet.

'Take a flat one, like this,' says Alfie, picking up a disc-shaped pebble near his feet. 'Then you lean back, aim, shout, "Fly, filibuster, fly," and you skim it – see?' Alfie's stone zips across the waves, four leaps in a row, before disappearing into the depths.

'I'm not saying that out loud. It's a stupid word.'

'Then it won't work,' he tells me.

'Yeah, right,' I mutter, selecting my weapon, leaning back, aiming and flicking my wrist. The stone leaves my hand, travels no more than three metres, and plops straight down into the shallows.

'Told you,' he says quietly, shaking his head.

'That's ridiculous,' I reply. 'You've just had more practice.'

Alfie shrugs.

'OK. Have it your way. Fly fili-whatever-you-are, fly.' I hurl my next missile. It arcs into the inky sky and drops into the sea. I raise my arms in a silent question.

'You've got to really shout,' Alfie explains. 'A filibuster is an adventurer, a troublemaker, a pirate. Think of the stone as his weapon, which he is hurling to escape capture. Fly, filibuster, fly!' he yells, this time spinning in a circle before launching his missile. I watch open-mouthed as a stone as large as a brick bounces off the water eight times.

'Fine,' I say through clenched teeth. I find the flattest, most aerodynamic pebble I can, take aim like an Olympic javelin champ and throw. 'Fly, filibuster, fly!' I scream, with all the passion in my heart. I know what it feels like to want to evade capture, after all. Alfie winces and covers his ears with his hands. The stone skims once and plummets into the water.

'I've had enough of this,' I sulk.

'You have to yell, then throw,' Alfie points out.

'Let's do it together. Here's a stone. After three. One, two, three . . .'

'Fly, filibuster, fly!' we screech, in unison, before hurling our pebbles. They skim three times in synchronicity, like dragonflies, and, where they sink, ripples fan out across the surface.

Alfie gives me a high five. I still think it's a lot of rubbish. But sometimes you just have to trust.

Chapter Twenty

I've never thrown a house-warming party before – in fact, I've never had any sort of party before. It's always just me and Mum for my birthday and we celebrate Thai-style. In Thailand, people are given fish or birds to release, one for every year of their lives and one extra for the year to come. Little Bird usually makes me paper birds. We bless them with water and then take them to the park, releasing them to the wind.

'*Suk san wan keut*,' my mother calls after them, waving. 'Happy birthday.' Then we go to the waffle bar for something extra special. Dad doesn't come because he says birthdays are a waste of time and who wants to celebrate getting older?

Today isn't about the day I was born, though. I want my new home to be full of good energies, so I've

laid string round the edge of the space like monks do when they are blessing a dwelling. It's supposed to help you think about how everything is connected. The ends meet on an altar, where I've put my chubby Buddha, some plastic flowers and some berries from a bush in the hospital grounds. It should be lotus flowers really, but I'm making do.

It's an exclusive event. The guest list only has two names on it. You can guess who they are.

Alfie is standing outside my front door singing 'Why Are We Waiting?'. I've told him he can't come in until everything is ready. Looking around, I'm proud of what we've achieved together. This is the first time Alfie will see the place neat and tidy, though. I've tried to make it cosy. There's a heavy beach towel hanging over the missing pane of our entry and exit point to stop the wind whistling in, and tea-light candles are warming the space with a yellow glow.

In honour of the occasion, I've even tied my hair back with a flower clip which matches the long purple

cardie I found in a charity-shop rummage box. 'Freakin'
Friday,' the man behind the counter said when he saw
me. I must admit, I look pretty weird most of the time.
As the days are getting colder, I'm adding more layers.

'You do what you have to do to survive,' Crease
told me. I know that now. I used to be sad that Dad
wouldn't let me paint my room green. Now I'm just
grateful for a roof over my head and every single
precious thing around me that I've collected.

My favourite piece of treasure is the orange and gold
material I discovered wrapped on a roll at the rubbish
tip. There was enough of it to make two sets of curtains
for my windows and a cushion cover. They wouldn't
win any prizes for needlework but the way their threads
sparkle in the light like tiny stars is awesome.

'What are you doing in there – painting a mural?'
Alfie sighs outside the door.

'Keep your hair on. One more minute, promise.'
Everything looks set. There's one last thing to do. I
reach for a red and gold plastic box with a figure of an

Indian bride and groom on top and open the lid.

A tinny back-beat starts to pulse and then there is a surprisingly loud 'ya na, ya ya ya' intro. An upbeat Bollywood pop song kicks in, filling the café. The bride and groom are spinning. I open my cardboard front door with a flourish. Alfie is making animal shadows on the wall with his fingers in time to the music. He starts to jiggle, moving his head from side to side. He motions for me to join him.

'I don't know the steps,' I protest.

'Mum's got a bhangra exercise DVD. Just do what I do,' says Alfie, taking my hand.

I follow his moves and we dance round the café, into the corridor and along to the reception, which is in almost pitch darkness. When the track ends, I have to run back to close and open the lid again, so we can carry on with our crazy dance. After about ten repetitions, the batteries of the music box have died and we're both out of breath, hot and giggly.

'Yabradabradoodle,' Alfie exclaims, when I lead

him into my house and he sees the transformation. '*Waay!*' He gives me a high five.

'You're learning Thai. I'm impressed,' I say.

'It's a cool crib, Caly.' Alfie whistles as he looks around.

'Arctic, more like.' I make shivering motions to back up my point. 'Better than a doorway or a wheelie bin, though. And it's detached, with a garden.'

'In the Middle Ages, it would have been luxurious,' Alfie says.

'Exactly. I'm queen of all I survey. For now,' I add, because who knows what's round the corner and whether it has fangs?

Nee seua bpa jo-ra-kay, kon dee. Escape from the tiger and into the crocodile, sweetheart.

'You could come and live with me, if you like.' Alfie is giving me a strange look, reading my fears.

'What would your mum say?' I ask. I think I already know the answer. Kid on the run equals major trouble.

Alfie shrugs. 'She'd like it if I weren't on my own.'

He's just saying that to be kind and there's probably some truth in it, but there's no way she wouldn't try to deliver me back to my parents, or haul me off to the authorities. If I were sixteen, I could make my own decisions. But being thirteen doesn't amount to a beetle in a banyan tree. I'm not ready for the first and I'll never be ready for the second.

Even so, it's the only really nice thing that anyone has said to me in ages. I do something unexpected, and give Alfie a hug. He looks surprised, embarrassed and pleased all at the same time.

'Babe magnet,' he says.

'Dream on.' I let go of him quickly. We are both looking anywhere but at each other.

I remember the last time I hugged Little Bird. The image of it has taken me by surprise. I can see us both crying. And there is pain in my side. It isn't distant, like the memory, but very real, very here and now.

'Do you miss home?' Alfie asks, out of the blue.

He's doing it again, the telepathy thing, which is too spooky.

'Some things so much it hurts,' I confide. 'My mum . . .' I begin, then have to break off because of the lump in my throat.

'She'll be missing you,' Alfie says, giving me another strange look, almost as if he knows what I am about to say.

'I went back to make sure she was OK. Couldn't go in, though, in case the FISTS had set a trap. I saw her through the window. She seemed to sense me there and came outside. I just wanted to put my arms round her. She was talking to herself, saying weird things. And there was a cop there.' I'm finding it hard to continue. Tears are welling up in my eyes.

'What's your mum like?' Alfie asks, holding my gaze.

'Little – no, tiny. Really pretty. Black hair. Almond eyes. A small mouth, like a rosebud. Cheek bones which curve in a smile. The smallest feet, honest to God, I don't know how she stands up. And she's got

this great laugh, like birds singing,' I tell him. *A laugh I would give anything to hear again.*

'Must be fun to come from two places in the world,' Alfie observes.

'Never really thought about it like that. It sort of feels like I don't really belong anywhere,' I try to explain. 'I'd love to go to Thailand and meet my other family. Don't suppose it'll ever happen, though. Not if my dad has anything to do with it.'

'He didn't buy her over the Internet, did he?' Alfie asks. He's hit on a raw point with Little Bird.

'No, course not! She met him on a snowy day in London, in the Bricklayers' Arms pub, six weeks after arriving in England and eight weeks after giving all her savings to a European man who promised her a job and a chance to study in the UK.' I tell the story of how Dad thought she was the most beautiful woman he had ever seen, how she fell for his flattery when he said he would help her. She found out later that Dad had made a bet with his friend the barman that he

could marry her before the month ended. He won five hundred pounds.

Never trust a promise.

'At least he hung around. Mine did a runner, or something,' says Alfie. 'Mum hasn't a clue where he is. Don't think she cares now.'

'Parents,' I groan.

'Better off without them sometimes.' Alfie is watching me. I know he's noticed that I'm shivering. It isn't with the cold, but the sudden recollection of a sequence of events: the sound of breaking glass; Little Bird screaming and telling me to run; me, leaving through our back door in the kitchen and sprinting up the side passage, away into the night. Sirens wailing, in the distance.

'Funny things, memories,' Alfie says quietly. I nod. He's reading my mind again, I could swear. 'Some of them are best left behind.'

'What do you mean?' I ask.

'Sometimes it's best not to know about the past.

158

Your mind blanks it off for a reason,' he says.

'I have to know what happened, Alfie. Until I do, I'm stuck here, in limbo. I don't know what to do for the best. Keep hiding? Go home? The answers are somewhere in here,' I tell him, hitting my skull with my knuckles. 'My stupid brain won't let them out.'

'You'll find the key, when you're ready,' Alfie says, sounding very certain. He has picked up a small power ball from my shelf and is bouncing it on the floor. He knows I won't be able to resist trying to grab it from him. I think he's trying to cheer me up.

He runs away from me and escapes into the garden. I'm hot on his tail.

He stands by the wall, throwing the ball from hand to hand. I have an idea. I run at him, leap, let my feet walk up the bricks, then push off and land perfectly, snatching the ball from the air. A sharp pain stabs my left leg. Worth it, though.

'Where did you learn that?' Alfie is dead impressed.

'Friend of mine. A free runner. I'll teach you if you like.'

Alfie doesn't respond. He's concentrating on catching me out. We dodge round each other while I'm bouncing the ball. Alfie tries to intercept it. I feel really light on my feet, even though it hurts to move. Must be fitter than I thought. Crease was right when he said free running is all about expressing yourself through motion. My body language is telling Alfie he's lost this contest. I do a forward flip just to prove the point.

'OK. You win.' Alfie shrugs and grins, but I notice his eyes aren't smiling.

Chapter Twenty-one

Round and round and round to the left. Round and round and round to the right. My eyes are mesmerised by the bundle of clothes and bedding curling over and over, like gymnasts performing a series of front and back flips.

The motion of the machine and the heat are making me sleepy, even though night has turned into day. A launderette is a strange place to be at six thirty a.m., but with ice on the inside of the café windows this morning, and my washing stiff and wet on my indoor line, I had to do something. I can't face spending another minute with my head on a damp pillow and my body shivering under covers growing mildew.

I found just enough money in the slots of parking machines to pay for one cycle of the tumble dryer. I'm

hoping that will be enough. It's been worth the price to sit here, soaking up the warmth and letting my brain unfreeze its thoughts. There's no one to disturb me, apart from a woman who works here, pottering in the back office, and the soothing voice of a male radio presenter, burbling between soft, morning music.

'And the news headlines from two-one-oh FM,' he announces. 'Juan Belaval, the European president, is calling for a freeze on immigration and foreign travel and warns that a state of emergency is only days from being announced. He says the escalation of the virus in Europe means that hospitals in many major cities have no more beds available. Representatives from all EU countries are in Brussels today to debate the health crisis. In London, stock-market floors are silent as several hundred traders are quarantined. And five hundred schools throughout the UK are facing temporary closure due to staff shortages.'

That's several thousand kids who will have a smile on their faces, I'm thinking. Every cloud has a silver

lining. I'm wondering if my school is closing and try to imagine the anticipation in Crease's eyes as an empty day stretches ahead of him. I'm hoping that Alfie might not have school either and that his mum will be cool with the idea of him visiting a friend.

'More news,' I hear the DJ say. 'The Association of Veterinary Surgeons has reported record numbers of owners requesting euthanasia for their pets, as more councils implement a programme of culling wild and domestic animals found on the streets after curfew. A decision on an escalation of the slaughter of farm animals is expected from the Department of Agriculture later this week.'

'That really gets my goat,' says the launderette assistant, standing in the doorway of the office, a plastic basket of washing in her hands. She has bright purple-red hair, a lined face like a scrunched crisp packet and a green apron over jeans and pink trainers. She reminds me of those puzzles where you put different heads and clothes on bodies and legs. 'Why should the poor

animals suffer? Seems to me it's the politicians who should be rounded up. Them's got us into this mess.'

I have a fleeting image of Furball hopping happily in the grounds of the hospital. It will be a miracle if she escapes capture. I realise the woman is looking at me intently. I suppose it must look odd – a kid drying her washing at this time of day. I've got my alibi ready; how our machine at home is broken and I'm doing this for my disabled mum, blah blah.

'Don't mind me,' says the woman, smiling. 'Stupid old Maisie is always talking to herself. Didn't hear you come in, love. Sorry. Did you manage to sort yourself out?'

'Yes, thanks,' I answer. My brain isn't up for a full conversation.

'Right you are,' Maisie says, bundling her pile of washing into a machine, closing the door and pressing a button. There is a whirr and a chug, like the sound of a train pulling out of a station, as the load starts to turn.

'Been here for thirty years and this is the worst

nonsense I've ever heard,' she continues, motioning at the radio. 'Breaks your heart when you think about all them dear little creatures being put down for nothing. This bug could have been sent to us for all we know, from one of those funny countries in the East. They're no friends of ours, mark my words.'

She catches my reaction to this comment. 'Sorry, love,' she apologises. 'No offence intended. Pretty little thing, aren't you, under all those funny clothes? Got your own style. Apple of your dad's eye, I shouldn't wonder.'

Yeah, right, if I were a greyhound or a race horse, I'm thinking, but I just smile back. I'm bending and stretching my bad leg too. The muscles keep threatening to go into spasm, now I've come in from the cold.

'Gets my goat, cramp,' Maisie sympathises. 'Used to get it rotten of a morning.' She whistles.

'It's OK now. Nearly,' I tell her. 'I hurt it, but it's mending.'

Maisie stops folding towels for a moment and gazes at me thoughtfully, like I'm an exhibit inside a glass case in a museum. I shift in my chair, uncomfortable.

'Friends are what count in this life, that's what I always think,' she says, her voice lowered. 'You got someone looking out for you, dear?'

'Yeah,' I answer, a bit hesitantly. Not that it's any of her business. I'm not sure I like where this conversation is going.

'Pleased to hear it,' says Maisie, nodding. 'Not much fun on your lonesome. I should know.' She's touching on the truth and it feels like we're on the dangerous edge of something.

'Don't you have friends?' I ask, to deflect the line of questions.

'Had three husbands,' she replies. 'Put them all together and they didn't even make one good one.' She gives me a big smile. 'Not so easy making friends these days. I meet lots of folks, but they're passing through, mostly.'

The timer on the drying machine gives three sharp beeps to indicate it has finished its cycle. I open the door and put my hand in. The sleeping bag and jeans are still very damp.

'Don't worry, love,' says Maisie, behind me. 'Another half hour should do it.' She puts a pound coin from her apron pocket in the slot, sets the dial and the belly of the machine starts to tumble again.

'I can't pay you back,' I say, embarrassed.

'Doesn't make no odds. What's a little kindness between friends?' Maisie winks at me and returns to folding towels and sheets at the counter. 'We girls have to stick together.'

I get the feeling she knows more about me than I've told her and I'm scanning the street outside in case there is a screech of cop cars or the sudden arrival of a van load of FISTS. Maisie could have called someone when she was in the office. But it's just getting light outside and nothing is moving, not even any traffic.

I'm on my guard, though, and I'm not reassured by

Maisie's cheery humming as she goes about her work. I keep my head in a magazine and my ears on red alert until the timer beeps again.

Then I'm up and stuffing the warm and dry belongings into two carrier bags before you can say *laiw jer gan* – see ya. I feel bad that I've been suspicious of Maisie after her kindness. Rude kids probably get her goat, so I go up to the counter where she's busy sorting a pile of dirty washing into darks and whites.

'Thanks again.' I meet her deep green eyes.

'Don't mention it, love. I do go on a bit. Don't often get the chance to chat – you know how it is. You take care, now.' With that, she disappears into the back office. And I leave the cosy warmth of the launderette for the ice-cold world outside.

Chapter Twenty-two

Bam, bam, bam, bam. We're running up a flight of steps, our feet moving fast over the concrete. It's hard to race and laugh at the same time. Alfie is yodelling and it's cracking me up. I'm only just ahead of him. We reach the top of the car park together and – *thud bang!* – we push through the fire door, which crashes back against a wall, and – *waay!* – we're out into the early morning air. We're on the eighth floor. There are no cars parked. It's just a huge space with railings and walkways. Perfect!

'You have to make your moves as fluid as you can, like running water,' I explain, when we get our breath back.

'Uh-huh,' says Alfie.

He was waiting for me when I got back to the hospital with my laundry, and said we should do

something fun before the world woke up. His school is closed for staff training so we can have the whole day together.

'So, what's he like, your friend?' Alfie is doing some strange air punching moves and running on the spot.

'Crease? Mega cool,' I reply. 'He could leap from here to that roof over there, no trouble.'

'No way.'

'He says you can do anything if you let your spirit and your body work as one.' I'm bending my legs in turn and stretching out, warming my muscles ready for action. I'll need to be extra careful with my bad leg. 'The only real obstacles are in your head. If you look at everything around you — streets, steps, buildings — everything can be a playground.'

'With no safety net,' Alfie points out.

'You'll be fine. Loosen your hamstrings and your shoulders.' I show Alfie what to do. He copies me, but exaggerates the moves. I start to giggle but his expression is serious.

'Fluid, like water, that's what you said.' He is trying to focus like an athlete. It makes me giggle even more.

'Yeah. But there's something else you have to do before we start.' I point at his trainers.

'Not bare feet?' He pulls a face.

I shake my head. 'Laces.'

Alfie bends over to tie them. 'Yeah, yeah, double knots, I know. You're as bad as my mum.'

We're all set. My heart is starting to race with excitement. We set off at a jog round the perimeter. We run forwards, backwards. We hang from railings, drop down and do body rolls.

Start slow, stay low. That's right, isn't it, Crease?

I show Alfie some special moves: a precision jump with no run-up, a monkey vault over some railings, a cat leap on to the roof of the pedestrian exit. My action isn't smooth, more like a tap spluttering into life, but it feels great to be moving after so many hours of each day cooped up at the hospital. It's like reconnecting with myself, the Caly Summer who wasn't a MISYO.

I don't want to stop now.

'Let's just go for it, Alfie. There are no rules. Just do it however you want.'

'OK,' he answers, flipping himself up into a handstand on railings and staying there.

'Whooooah! Pretty good for a beginner.' I give him a round of applause. He wobbles and lands in a heap on the ground.

'I've got a good teacher,' he grins. I remember saying the same thing to Crease. It didn't please him.

Use your body to say things your way, Paper Clip. Make art, make a statement, make a protest. It's up to you. It's your right. You might run with the Feathers, but you are an individual, you get me? An' when you put all that cre-a-tivity together, you get somethin' more powerful than a river. It's a tidal wave. An' the System can't stop it.

'C'mon, Alfie,' I shout, taking off at speed and using as many different moves as possible to get me to the floor below. In a moment, Alfie is next to me. We balance on concrete blocks, then leap the big gap

to the next level, rolling on impact. Alfie has picked this up really fast. He's a natural. And he's adding some twists to his jumps and turns. He sees me staring at him, quizzically.

'I went to gym club until I was nine. My pre-muffin phase,' he grins, squidging his belly between two fingers.

'You should still do it. You're really good.'

'Nah. Parallel bars or chocolate bars — it's a no-brainer.'

Alfie's moving ahead of me now. I get the feeling the topic of his gym club days is closed.

We're on the last ramp near the entrance, running at full speed, but there's a blue sports car accelerating towards us, taking no notice of the five-mile-an-hour speed-limit sign. I cling to the side of the concrete wall but the crazy male driver doesn't slow down.

'Alfie!' I yell, and in a split second he leaps and clears the top of the car, landing on both feet. The car's brakes screech at the top of the ramp and the vehicle

stops with its engine running. The driver gets out.

'You should get off the ramp,' he says in a loud voice. His words are slightly slurred. I notice his tie is loose round his neck and his suit is rumpled.

'And you shouldn't drive like a banana head,' I shout back. He looks as if he's about to stride towards us, but then he seems to stumble and change his mind. He gets back in the car, slamming the door. The car moves off, the roar of its engine echoing through the building.

The man's outburst has reminded me of something. My head is filled with noise – a series of angry words – *Come here . . . did you hear me? Come here.* In my mind, it's the drunk driver yelling them at us, but that doesn't make any sense. In a flash they have gone and I'm looking at Alfie, who is on all fours.

'Are you OK?' I ask, walking over to him.

'Wow. Omigod. Yeah. That was, um, *really* cool. Kicking, in fact,' Alfie answers, his eyes wide with terror and exhilaration. His whole body is trembling.

'You're not supposed to get yourself killed, OK?' I'm hugging him really tight.

'I think I'm fairly indestructible, don't worry,' he replies. He lifts his sweat shirt and reveals his Superman T-shirt. 'And, anyway, I've seen them do it on *Dare Devils*. A stunt man jumped a moving limo . . .'

'Alfie?' My body is trembling now. I nearly lost my best friend. 'Shut up.'

Chapter Twenty-three

'Trick or treat,' says a croaky voice outside my front door. It sounds like a cross between a frog and an old woman. I'm not scared. I've been expecting it. In fact, I've even dressed up for the occasion in an orange wool hat and scarf, black jacket and jumper and green cord trousers, held up with braces.

I pull back the cardboard and my mouth drops open. Standing before me is a black blob with star lights festooned around it. They blink every few seconds. The blob's face is obscured by a plastic mask with eye, nose and mouth slits and smothered by curtains of shoulder-length hair.

In its hands, which are covered with black gloves, the blob is holding a pumpkin which has a loose lid and no features.

'Freakin' Friday,' I exclaim.

'I'm a black hole, in case you're wondering,' says the blob. *Blink blink*, go the lights.

'Kicking hair, Alfie – sorry, black hole.'

'Used Mum's straighteners,' he says. 'Can I come in? This pumpkin weighs a ton.'

He shuffles inside, *blink blink*, and puts the large orange ball on the table.

'Can you take the mask off now? It's a bit creepy.'

Alfie is shaking his head. 'Do you feel the gravitational pull?' he asks, holding his arms out towards me.

Blink blink.

'Nice try. The lights are good,' I say. 'What are they running off?'

'Personality,' he answers. I can't see if he's grinning. He can't see me pull a face. He lifts up his jumper revealing a round moon of a belly and a battery pack stuck to his skin with brown tape. The movement sends the lights into manic mode.

'Uh-oh,' says Alfie. 'Cyber meltdown.' He hits the pack with his fist and the lights die. 'I've killed the universe – I am all powerful,' he bellows, making me jump.

With his mask off, he looks like a girl. I can't stop staring at his hair. It's longer than mine.

'Did you see your mates before coming here?' I ask. Alfie said he'd had another invitation for tonight and I had my fingers crossed that he would decide mine was the better option.

'Nah. Didn't fancy watching *Night of the Purple Slayers* and sticking my face in a bowl of green jelly. Anyway, they're out trick or treating.'

'We could do that,' I suggest. It's the one night of the year when calling on strangers is allowed. I can join in without anyone suspecting I'm a missing kid. Everyone else will be wearing a wardrobe from Hell too.

'Curfew's in an hour,' warns Alfie. 'And, anyway, people won't answer their doors.'

'It will be fun seeing all the costumes,' I plead.

'Well . . .'

'Yabradoodle!' I say, before he has a chance to say yes or no.

I'm eager to rush straight out, but Alfie is taking ages putting his mask on again. What's got into him tonight?

'I'm going to blow out the candles,' I say, when I can't stand it any longer.

I extinguish the last of the tea lights and pull my scarf up over half my face for anonymity.

I open the cardboard door and we are just about to set off on our adventure when Alfie stops in his tracks and grabs my arm.

'What is it?' I whisper. Then I hear it too – the unmistakable sound of voices.

'Visitors,' says Alfie. 'Get the torch.'

I fumble around in the dark until my fingers find it on my bookcase. They wrap round its handle and I hold it close to my thumping heart.

'What are we going to do?' I ask, panic building.

'Stay calm. They might just go away. But if they come in, shine the beam in their eyes and hold it there.'

'The lights have gone out, look,' says a girl, just a few metres from where we're standing.

'Double dare you to go in.' It's a boy's voice this time. There is a babble of excitement – it must be a big group. My hand reaches for Alfie's and grips it tightly.

He squeezes it back and puts a finger to his lips to remind me to be silent. Every part of me is trembling, even my ears.

'What do I get if I do it?' the girl asks. She's flirting with him. The crowd is jeering and cheering. They sound like my dad when he comes home from the pub – loud and argumentative.

'You'll find out if you do it,' says the boy. 'But you've got to come out with a trophy.'

'Give me your blade, then,' answers the girl.

'Mind, it's sharp.'

'Unlike your brain.' More jeering from the group.

There is a scrabbling outside the window, laboured

breathing, and the scrape of a shoe with a heel as it lands on the floorboards inside the café.

'I can't see anything,' the girl complains. 'Anyone got a lighter?'

'Yeah, Harry has, but he's too much of a girl to go in,' calls another boy.

'Watch out for the Undead, Steph,' yells the first one.

'Will you shut it?' the girl inside the café – Steph – replies. She is moving towards my house, placing one foot carefully after another. I can imagine her hands reaching out to feel for anything solid, tracing across my wall of books, pushing at my flimsy front door. I feel sick and faint. Discovery is inevitable.

'Oh fag boxes!' Steph exclaims. There is a thud and the sound of metal hitting against metal. I grimace. The scooters! I left them outside the house, propped up against the wall.

'You all right, Steph?' calls the boy.

I can hear snorts of laughter and stones clattering against the top window panes.

'Something weird here,' Steph replies. Her breathing is closer now. Her hands have started to explore the wall blocking her way. My finger is on the torch's switch. My heart is in my mouth.

'Some sort of den, made of books,' she says quietly to herself.

'Hurry up, Steph, Harry needs a dump,' calls a voice. Loud laughter. 'Too late! Harry, that's disgusting.'

'You can be my trophy,' Steph says, pulling at a hardback by the side of the front door. Any minute now, the wall will collapse. Any moment now, a teenager with a knife is going to get the surprise of her life.

Alfie has let go of my hand and picked up the pumpkin shell. He is holding it above his head.

'Steph, come on, it's time to get out of here,' yells the first boy.

'Just getting a trophy,' Steph shouts back, tugging at the book.

'Forget it,' calls the boy, more agitated. 'This is getting boring.'

'Don't waste your time, Steph,' calls another voice.

'Got it,' Steph shouts triumphantly. It's a miracle, but the wall doesn't come tumbling down round our ears, and the intruder begins to move away. Alfie lowers the pumpkin and I can hear him start to breathe out, relieved.

Blink blink. His star lights flash. The two of us go rigid. Steph gasps.

Blink blink. Alfie is hitting the battery pack, but it's no good.

Blink blink. The cardboard door is suddenly flung open. Steph stands in the space, her eyes narrowed in a frown of determination, a long-bladed knife held out in front of her. In the same moment, I click on the torch and shine it directly at her face. We both scream. Alfie launches the pumpkin, which hits her on the head with a thud. She staggers back, dropping the blade.

'Robbie!' she screams, making for the window,

stumbling over the scooters for a second time. I switch the beam off again.

'Steph?' the boy calls.

'Robbie!' she whimpers this time. By now she is out of the café and back in the grounds. 'There's someone in there. But all I could see was this blinding light.'

'Don't matter now. We've got to cut. It's after eight,' says the boy. 'Still, no trophy, no prize.'

'You're such a skank, Robbie Nuttall.' Steph's voice is almost an octave higher than before.

The group is moving away now. I hear feet on gravel, laughter fading. Alfie and I are still rooted to the spot in the dark. Several minutes pass and we don't speak, just in case it's a trap. Just in case the teenagers have attracted the attention of the FISTS.

'I think it's OK,' says Alfie at last, removing his mask. I click the torch on again, aiming it at the floor to reduce its brightness.

'That was close.' I pick up the knife. Its blade is about twenty centimetres long. In that second, for no

reason, I feel a searing pain in my bad leg and my head is filled with flashing images of my mother, screaming and blood. Blood everywhere. Over her. Over me. And she's yelling at me to run. But I'm throwing myself at her, hugging her, not wanting to let her go and we're both crying and she is pushing me away.

I'm suddenly on my knees, and it's hard to breathe.

'I don't understand,' I keep repeating.

'You will,' Alfie says gently. He's sitting on the ground next to me, an arm round my shoulders. His lights are still blinking every few seconds and it's hard to take his earnest gaze seriously.

'What do you mean? How do you know?' I ask him. I know he's just saying things to make me feel better.

'Everyone does, in the end,' he says matter of factly. I'm about to tell him to stop trying to be so smart when a loud bang sends a shudder through the whole frail building. It's like a drill hitting concrete. It reverberates and echoes. Then it happens again. The noise seems to be coming from the street outside the

grounds. Its beat is insistent, slow and menacing.

'We should check it out,' says Alfie.

'You're still blinking. I'll go.'

Alfie fumbles under his top and tries to rip the wire out of the battery pack. It sticks. In frustration, he grabs the knife and cuts through it.

'Sorted.' He motions for me to turn the torch off before we venture from the café.

Once in the grounds, we run as quietly as possible across the overgrown lawn, through the wild borders to the pillars by the entrance where the griffins roar silently into the night. I'm impressed by how lightly Alfie moves, like a free runner, hardly making a sound. The ground is trembling with each new bang, as if a drummer is sounding a march for an army of giants.

'Crikey Moses,' says Alfie, who is the first to take a peek round the pillar. He seems reluctant to move out of the way – in fact he's actively blocking me – so I do a mini cat leap and claw myself up the wall to get a better view.

'Caly, get down!' he whispers. 'It's too dangerous.'

'It's OK for you but not for me,' I mouth at him, waving my arms in frustration. Alfie reads my lips but just glares hard at me, giving out a low, warning growl.

BANG! Just a few metres away now, the noise is almost deafening.

I can't believe what I'm seeing. There must be fifty figures in full body suits and helmets, like storm troopers, marching in long lines on opposite sides of the pavement. They are holding large silver balls and twice a minute, in complete unison, they are bouncing them. In the centre of the road, another line of troops holds huge canisters, like fire extinguishers. Any minute now, I'm expecting someone to shout, 'Cut,' and for a film crew to appear, because surely, honest to God, this is not for real.

BANG! go the balls again.

'What are they doing?' I mouth to Alfie. He shrugs.

And then it becomes clear. The noise is flushing out the creatures of the night – the foxes, cats, stray

dogs, rabbits, rats and lost guinea pigs. As they run, disorientated, into the path of the troops, they are sprayed with gas from the canisters. Death is swift, but, from the amount of writhing, it isn't painless. Their bodies lie where they drop and a man jumps out of a white lorry following slowly behind to pick the corpses up and sling them in the back.

I slide down the wall and drop to the ground next to Alfie, who looks as shocked as I am.

'It's because of the virus,' he says.

'Maybe it is, maybe it isn't.' I imagine Crease telling me to keep that thought to myself. My fingers find the bottle top in my pocket and turn it over and over. What if the government's got it wrong and it's not animals spreading the disease? What if they know that, but they're killing them anyway? *That's the question you'd ask, isn't it, Dair?*

'There's nothing we can do,' Alfie says.

'There is.' As soon as the white lorry and the marching morons have disappeared from view, I run

into the street and scour the verges, front gardens and hedges for signs of life – for signs of any lucky creature which stayed hidden and saved its skin.

And most of all, for signs of Furball.

Chapter Twenty-four

'Come on,' says Alfie, tugging my sleeve. 'It'll be fun.'

Since Halloween, I haven't felt like going out, not even to search for Furball. I've needed to be quiet, to read and to think.

Alfie says I'm depressed. He might be right. There seems a lot to be sad about. There's stuff going on outside these walls that is plain wrong and I don't just mean the killing of animals. People aren't free to move around. Kids who fight the System are taken away. How many of them have microchips messing up their brains, like Dair?

I'm beginning to realise that I've lived with my eyes closed, in one place – the estate – never questioning how much the System controls everything. I didn't think about what was going on outside our zone at all

until I met Crease. I accepted things, did as I was told. Kept quiet about stuff that upset me.

Kids are often born into situations they wouldn't choose. It happens all over the world, every minute of every day. Why should it have been different for me? The important thing is to figure out a way to change things. Maybe hanging out with the Feathers was my first step.

A step on a path which has brought me here.

I'm feeling sorry for *myself* too. I'm a kid, living alone, in pain. I can't go home. My stupid brain won't let me remember why I ran away. I don't know what to do.

I've been racing through the books in my walls. They've been full of revelations, but no answers to my puzzles. I want to understand why things are happening, why animals are being murdered at night, why all of us have to stay indoors after eight o'clock, why children are being sent to the detention centre. I want to know why family rules can be just as restricting,

like a rope round your neck, pulling ever tighter.

I don't want to be silent now. The silence connects all the puzzles out there, allows them to happen.

All I know for certain is that for the last few weeks I've had new eyes, which don't like what they see. And a friendship which feels like home.

'Sooty, we'll miss the surprise,' says Alfie, snapping his fingers about two millimetres away from my face.

'Sorry.' I blink. We are holding each other's gaze deeply. I realise I'm spending more and more time each day thinking about Alfie. When he's this close, I go all tingly and my throat tightens up. He's swallowing hard and sniffing, so maybe we're allergic to each other. But if that were true I don't think it would feel this nice.

Suddenly, my house fills with bright light. There is a loud, crackling bang overhead and the harsh *rat-a-tat* of explosions like gunfire.

'Fireworks,' Alfie says, breaking the silence between us.

'Yes.' My head is nodding slowly. My breathing has become shallow and fast.

'We're missing them,' he persists, eye contact still fixed.

'Are they the surprise?' I forgot it's the Festival of Lights. My voice has gone weirdly husky.

Alfie shakes his head and launches into action. 'Put on every layer you've got,' he instructs. 'And an extra one for luck.'

Within minutes, we are scootering down the hill side by side, scarves trailing like the tails of comets. Above and all around, the night sky is exploding. The *BOOM* of gunpowder is followed by cascades of colour; fountains, spheres and domes, filling the horizon.

We hurtle past the leaning houses, the locked sweet shop, the launderette which still has its lights on and customers waiting for their washing. I catch a glimpse of Maisie, her hands on her hips, probably telling them about the latest thing that has 'got her goat'.

The coast road is closed for the aerial display and

is packed with crowds. There are little kids perched high on adult shoulders and rows of old people sat like sardines on benches or in electric buggies. The fireworks are lighting up their faces, hundreds of them, and all mouths seem to be open.

'Oooh!' they are exclaiming. 'Aaah,' they are sighing, according to the size of each explosion.

Safety in numbers, I'm thinking. No one is giving us a second glance. I'm looking at them, though, each and every one of them, in case under a woolly hat or a hood or a pair of ear muffs I recognise the long, flowing, perfumed locks and drawn features of Dair.

The more I analyse it, the more I believe I might be the cause of his disappearance. Did he think I had abandoned him, when I had really gone to find help? Did he set fire to the building in anger or desperation? Alfie says it was just to do with his madness. Did it happen because I'd let Dair down? Perhaps I brought the bad luck with me to the hospital. Maybe, like Gran says, it's a bad penny you can carry in your pocket.

KaBOOM go the rockets, over our heads, raining sparks like confetti. Alfie is enjoying this. His eyes are bright with wonder and excitement. He looks like a kid who has never seen the dark side of life. I feel guilty suddenly. By being friends with me, he is risking so much. He's lying to his mum, for starters. He's staying up really late most nights and going home to his bed in the early hours. His schoolwork must be suffering, although he never says. He's even smuggled out some of his mum's old clothes.

He's done all this for me. He looks out for me, but he isn't pushy. I feel I can tell him anything and he won't be angry, or make fun of me, or say vicious things. He gets impatient if I talk about Dair, but that's probably because he's being protective. Dair is trouble, in his opinion. Maybe I am trouble for Alfie. I can't bear the thought of anything happening to him because of me and my bad penny.

'How's your leg?' Alfie asks, out of the blue.

'Good,' I answer. 'Sore in the mornings and last

thing, like someone's sticking a needle in. But it goes away. Why?'

'Wondered if you'd like a better view?' He nods towards a circle of light in the distance. 'It'll be quite a push, though,' he adds.

'What is it?'

'A big wheel,' Alfie answers. 'The fair always comes for the festival night.'

'I've never been to a fair, or ridden on a big wheel,' I admit. I've never even seen the one that comes to our zone once a year. My dad says it's the place where lowlives wait to prey on girls like me and he doesn't want me wasting exit tokens on going somewhere so dangerous.

Little Bird told me not to say that Crease and Slee go there and win stuffed toys and coconuts on the shooting gallery.

From here, the fair doesn't look dangerous. The wheel is beautiful, an arc of blue, green and pink lights.

'So, do you feel up to it?' asks Alfie, concerned.

'Yabradoodle,' I reply, with a smile. I'm going to try to be cheerful, for Alfie's sake.

The ride along the coast road to the fairground takes us about ten minutes. We dodge around groups of kids waving light-sticks and luminous neck haloes. We give a wide berth to the teenagers throwing Chinese fire-crackers on the ground.

Alfie weaves between the tall legs of a stilt walker – he can be such an idiot – and nearly gets us both run over by six unicycles, travelling in pairs, following just behind. They don't bother to slow down for us so we have to zigzag out of their way.

I've got hiccups from laughing so hard. I'm glad we came out. I didn't realise firework night was so much fun. It's taking my mind off my aching thigh.

The music from the fair gets louder as we approach. The beats from all the different rides are competing with each other. There are screams of fear coming from the roller coaster and the hammer, which swings a full three hundred and sixty degrees. There are bleeps and

sirens blasting from the bumper cars and a thousand other noises, human and electronic, combining to create the loudest discord I've ever heard.

Lasers are criss-crossing in the sky like chopsticks. Round, coloured lights outside the stalls flash in sequence.

'Roll up, roll up!' shout the men and women with money belts strapped to their waists, eager for the visitors to part with their cash. 'Win a prize, sir, win a prize, madam. Three goes for a fiver, you can't say fairer than that.'

This is a world away from curfew and the killing squads. It's like another country, one which isn't in the grip of a deadly disease. The rules about staying in are relaxed tonight and people have spilled from their houses like lab rats uncaged. Young women in short skirts and high heels are letting gravity hurl them round and round and upside down. Kids are stuffing their faces with candyfloss and dancing in front of mirrors that distort your shape. Mums and dads are parting

with twenty pound notes as if someone has told them it's the end of the world.

Scan, Caly. Plan your escape route, just in case.

Outside the ring of neon lights, there is just darkness. The firework display has ended and now the air is heavy with smoke and the acrid smell of explosives. I'm thinking that when the festivities end there won't be much time to reach the hospital before the curfew.

'Isn't it great?' Alfie asks as we leave the scooters by the trunk of a large tree and make our way into the sea of bodies. He motions for me to follow him and we push against the tide of movement towards the eye in the sky. Now we are up close, it looks colossal. Its passengers are so far away when they are swept to the top of the arc that their faces are indistinct and their screeches like the distant howl of wolves.

There's a queue for the ride. Alfie counts heads, waits for six more people to join it, and then he and I tag on the end. It is only then I see the sign ahead

which says that the cost is three pounds. My excitement drops into my belly like a stone. There's no way we can pay. Alfie has read it too but isn't reacting.

'We haven't got six quid, dur,' I say, making a point.

'We won't need it.'

'You think we can get on without being noticed? What about that bald gorilla with huge muscles who's in charge of taking the money?'

Alfie nods and taps his nose. The big wheel has finished its rotations and passengers are being unloaded carriage by carriage and their places filled by the people in our queue. The couple in front of us are the last ones to be invited on to the platform and then gorilla man puts the chain across the entrance again. Alfie motions for me to slip under it before anyone notices, and we sneak along the wooden walkway, right to the end. There's an empty carriage between two full ones about half a metre from the ground and we have a split second to clamber on board, lifting the metal bar so that it wedges us into place.

'They leave one in every ten carriages free,' explains Alfie, puffing. 'So the weight is balanced.' He sees the look of concern on my face. 'Don't worry. We don't weigh much. At least, I don't,' he adds, and I use his chubby arm as a mock punch bag. Already, we've lifted several metres into the air as the carriages behind are filled.

The higher we ascend, the more the noise on the ground fades. At the top of the arc, there is only the winter wind, blowing whispers of classical music into the stratosphere. It's the 'Dance of the Sugar Plum Fairy'. I recognise it from my gran's CD collection. It's one of the tunes she always used to hum when she was washing up.

'There, the torchlight procession. We've got the best seats in the house,' says Alfie, pleased with himself.

Far below, about twenty Festival of Light societies in different costumes, from native tribes to Elizabethan courtiers, are marching behind brass bands and lines of drummers. They carry flaming torches and some are

dancing as they progress along the coast road.

Alfie joins in, which causes the carriage to rock violently and my eyes to grow as wide as saucers.

'They used to burn papier-mâché models at the end of the march,' he explains, taking no notice of my terror. 'Giant models of politicians, celebrities, religious dudes in dresses.'

Not Bud the Pud, I'm hoping.

Alfie continues. 'Mum says it's against the law now, for health and safety reasons. But she thinks the government just wanted it stopped because so many of the models looked like the prime minister or the European president.'

'Alfie?'

'What?'

'Can you stop jiggling? It's a really LONG WAY DOWN,' I plead.

'OK. Sorry. Hold on tight.'

As he says this, the wheel starts to rotate at full speed. My stomach lurches each time we skim the

ground and swoop back into the air. The rush of oxygen in my lungs and my brain feels electrifying. I'm gripping Alfie's arm for all I'm worth and I'm laughing because the wind has whipped his crazy hair into a ball of frizz.

'Alfie, I don't want this to end. I always want to feel this free!'

Alfie pauses for a second, then looks at me intently. 'Then there's something I need to tell you,' he replies. 'And it won't wait another day.'

Chapter Twenty-five

'Let's just escape over the ocean and find our very own island to live on,' I suggest.

'It'll have to be somewhere with a fun fair, where all the rides are free,' he answers.

We are sitting in a large, wooden fishing boat called the *Aurora*, on the shingle in front of a row of beach huts and messy tackle sheds. The boat is roped to a winch, which lowers it into the water at high tide and drags it back up the beach with its haul from the sea each morning, before the town has even stirred.

We are huddled out of the wind by the *Aurora*'s engine, wrapped in black bin liners we found at the fairground. It's after midnight. The parades and festivities have finished. The revellers have gone home. There is no noise, except for the whistle of the

wind between the huts and the sea smashing against the shore.

'Warm enough?' asks Alfie, pulling the plastic up over my exposed hand.

'Baking.' I smile, trying to stop my teeth chattering like a wind-up skull. I've never spent the night on the beach before and Alfie's plan for us to hang out and watch the sunrise is totally ace.

'You're a brilliant mate,' I tell him. 'No one's ever taken me anywhere special before.'

'You won't think that when you get hypothermia.' He's rubbing his nose, which probably means he's embarrassed.

'What happens when your mum comes home, though?' I ask.

'She's doing a longer shift tonight,' says Alfie. 'She likes us to have a few treats at Christmas.'

'She sounds really nice. Maybe I could meet her soon.'

'Yeah. Maybe,' replies Alfie. He's staring at the sea.

'I could see which footballers you've got on your wall,' I tease.

Alfie pulls a face. 'Do I look like a footie fan?'

I shrug. I realise I don't know much about him, despite all the time we've spent together. I don't like to think he is hiding stuff from me. Maybe I just haven't asked enough questions. 'OK. Another guess. Shelves of little painted soldiers?'

'Nope,' says Alfie, clearly enjoying this.

'Posters of wildlife, pop stars, cars, robots?' I'm grasping at straws now.

'Not even close. I like maps. Weird, I know. My dad was a geography teacher, so it must be in my genes.'

'Didn't he ever try to contact you?' I ask.

Alfie shakes his head. 'Mum paid a private detective to find him, but there was no trace. It was like he never existed. The tec said she should leave it and not ask any more questions.'

'I'm really sorry,' I say. My back teeth have decided they are so cold they will hit against each other twice a

second. I try to clamp my jaw shut.

'Tough on my mum. Think she gets lonely,' adds Alfie. He seems lost in thought.

'She's got you.' I nudge him, hoping to cheer him up a little. He just nods sadly. Now my eyes are stinging with the onset of tears, but they're not for Alfie's situation. I'm thinking about Little Bird, and how alone she must feel. I rub my face so that Alfie doesn't notice.

'I'm not much company, Caly.'

'Maybe you should stay home more, then?' That came out a bit snappy. I don't like the thought of seeing Alfie less often.

'That's not what I mean,' he says, rubbing a hand through his hair. 'I'm not –'

Suddenly a bright beam of light sweeps over the bow of the boat. Alfie and I hunker down even further by the engine, covering our faces. We try not to move a muscle.

The scooters. We left them by the fishing huts, one leaning against the other.

'Oscar One, I have two kids' scooters, eastern bay by the fishing boats. No sign of their riders. They might be stolen, or the owners might have decided to go for a festive swim, over,' says a deep voice into a radio handset. 'Request dog unit on the scene as soon as possible, over. Copy that Oscar One. Out.'

Jaws on paws. My body is trembling, not just with the cold. The light beam moves across the *Aurora*, more slowly this time, searching the nooks and crannies. Discovery is seconds away.

'After three, jump up, grab the net and throw it over him,' whispers Alfie. I nod, clenching my teeth together as hard as possible so that their chattering doesn't give us away.

'One, two . . .' begins Alfie. The beam sweeps across me, but then returns.

'Who's there?' shouts the man sternly.

'Three!' yells Alfie. We leap to our feet like two ninja warriors and rush forward, scooping up the rope netting on our way. A split second later, we are hurling

it over the head of the policeman, who is rushing towards us, a baton raised in one hand. He stumbles, thrashes around, and we leap off the boat on to the shingle, running as fast as we can to put a distance between ourselves and the *Aurora*. It's a shame about the scooters, but this isn't a game any more.

What's your plan, Paper Clip? To get out of here, Crease.

'They'll be looking for us now,' says Alfie, gasping. 'Better get away from the cameras.' Sure enough, there are sirens not too far away.

'It's OK, follow me,' I tell him.

We sprint across the coast road, slide between parked cars, jump metal gates and vault lightly over garden walls, until we emerge on to a side road bordered by trees. We're constantly checking behind us for the sign of a patrol car or a white FIST van. Getting captured isn't an option, not after everything. If Alfie is sent to the rehabilitation centre, it will probably break his mum's heart. I'm the bad penny.

And I'm going to cost him his chance of a normal life.

'Alfie, just leave me,' I call to him.

'Don't be stupid,' he replies, frowing.

'You don't need to get caught. It's me they want. I'm the runaway, remember?'

'Tough tarantulas,' he shouts, ahead of me.

'That's so dumb, Alfie.' But there isn't time to argue. My adrenaline is pumping. We seem to be covering the ground at super-fast speed. Before long, we reach the hill that rises towards the hospital and there is a patrol car parked halfway up, its blue lights flashing. Just pulling up behind it is a large, dark van. We can hear the muffled sound of dogs barking.

'We'll have to go through the gardens and down the alleys,' says Alfie. 'The dogs'll track us in no time if we stay on the pavement. Stick close to me, Caly, OK?'

We set off again at a fast jog, jumping walls, running over the tops of sheds, bunny-hopping fences. Alfie isn't even panting. I'm the one who's out of breath,

fighting a stitch which is threatening to cut my upper belly in two.

'Keep going,' he encourages. I manage a small smile to reassure him. But then, overhead, there is the ominous noise of blades slicing through air. It's a bug, approaching fast, a bright beam lighting everything in its path.

'Along here,' says Alfie, taking us into a narrow alley which runs between two houses. 'Keep your head down.'

The alley leads to a labyrinth of rough paths around the back of the houses, some filled with garden refuse, others blocked by old mattresses or washing machines. There is even a Shetland pony tethered in one, munching something in a bucket. It makes a small disgruntled noise in its throat as we pass. I feel so sorry for it. The owner must be trying to hide it from the killing squad.

The path leads to a high wooden fence – the dead end we were dreading. While Alfie hesitates, I increase my speed and leap, attempting to scale it with a running

climb, just like the Feathers would. Just like Slee did, that day at the Town Hall. I'm on top and down the other side before you can say 'jumping bean'.

How's that, Crease? I'm one of the gang now.

Alfie is by my side before I can catch my breath. I look at him, surprised, impressed and very puzzled.

'Like I said, I'm a quick learner.' He shrugs.

I really want to quiz him, but the bug in the sky has fixed its gaze on the ground and is circling with its huge, white eye.

'In here,' says Alfie, half pushing me into a shed and closing the door behind us. The shed smells of petrol and, weirdly, chicken poo. A lawn mower takes up most of the space, but we manage to drop down on to the wooden floor, gratefully.

'That was so close,' I say.

Alfie is nodding. He rips off the black plastic liner and screws it into a ball. 'We'll stay here till the morning.'

'I might get to see the sunrise after all.' I smile. Alfie doesn't smile back. His face is fixed in concentration.

'How's your leg now?' he asks.

'Good,' I reply. 'Hardly a twinge.' Alfie doesn't seem pleased. He closes his eyes.

'Dair thought it was probably just a torn muscle,' I add. Alfie doesn't respond. 'You hate it when I talk about him, don't you?' I say. Alfie opens one eye and looks at me.

'Don't you?' I repeat. 'Are you jealous, or something?'

'No,' he answers quietly.

Check out every angle, Paper Clip. See it every which way.

I decide to leave the touchy subject of Dair. 'What is it you were going to tell me, anyway?'

'It's not the right time. I thought it was, but –' Alfie shrugs.

'Right time for what? I don't get it, Alfie. I tell you everything and you shut me out.'

'Sorry. I don't make the rules,' he says.

'What rules? You're talking rubbish.'

My brain is racing, throwing up questions. What if Dair's dead and Alfie knew all along? Why didn't I ever

think of this before? Suddenly, my mind is tumbling full of suspicion.

'Are you keeping stuff from me because you think I can't handle the truth?'

Alfie pulls his own hair in frustration. 'It's complicated, Caly.'

'What is? Look, I'm not a little kid. I'm a MISYO, in case you haven't noticed.'

'OK. OK. You and me. We're —' Alfie pauses, searching for a word.

'Just about to have a mega row,' I warn. I'm starting to lose it with my best mate.

'Different.'

'Yes, you're a boy and I'm a girl.' I wipe a large cobweb away from my face, crossly.

'More than that.'

'Are you ashamed of me, or something? Is that why you won't let me meet your mum? You never invite me over. If she's as nice as you make out, she wouldn't turn me in.'

'It's not that.' Alfie sounds hurt now.

'I think you just want to have me as your secret friend when she leaves you by yourself. You scared of the dark or something? Is that it? You just want someone to hold your hand?' That was mean. *Alfie, I'm so sorry.*

'You need to listen to what I'm saying,' says Alfie, anguish in his voice.

'So tell me about Dair, about the fire, about what really happened that day. You know things, don't you? I want the truth, Alfie, or we're history. And I'll be out of here, bug or no bug, before you can say –'

'I'm trying, Caly. But the rules . . .' he starts to explain.

'Oh my God, you're one of *them*, aren't you? And you know what? I think *you* started the fire.' I'm on my feet, turning the latch on the shed door, already feeling the rush of cold air on my face.

Chapter Twenty-six

I'm opening my eyes. Closing them. Opening them, just to make sure I'm not hallucinating. I've been sleeping for twelve hours – a black, cold, dreamless sleep, like being immersed in a tank of frozen chemicals.

I'm back in my house of books, lying on my bed, still wearing the black bin liner. The events of last night are filtering back into my consciousness: the big wheel, the fishing boat, the policeman; escaping, leaving the scooters behind. Running for our lives. Hiding from the bug in the sky.

An argument.

My chest tightens when I think of how angry I was with Alfie. The anger has subsided into hurt now. I don't understand his secrecy. I thought we were mates. We've spent all these weeks together and for the whole

time he's been holding something back. Something he doesn't want me to know, because he thinks it will change things between us forever.

It doesn't make any sense. He's just a thirteen-year-old kid, like me. Why did I think for a minute that he could have started the fire?

There are rules, he said. Yeah, Alfie, there are rules in friendship too. Number one, you don't keep secrets. And, in my book, mates come before rules anyway.

So now I have the puzzle of Alfie to add to the other puzzles. There are still so many pieces missing. I feel quite sick and when I touch my forehead, it is cool and clammy. Even the dull light coming though my curtains is hurting my eyes.

It could be a reaction to the overdose of adrenaline in my system that helped me duck and dive my way out of trouble each time the bug eye looked my way.

You would have been proud of me, Crease. I kept them guessing.

The alternative is that these are symptoms of the

virus. I don't even want to go there.

On top of all of that, anxiety for Alfie is gnawing at me like a starved rat. I don't know if he got home, back to his bedroom with maps on the wall. If he didn't, and he's in detention, should I tell his mum what happened? That I'm the bad penny who rolled into his life? Have the police got there already, with their harsh knock on the door and their rule book?

My thoughts are gathering momentum, whirling out of control. The big wheel in my mind has sheared off its axis. I can hear crowds screaming below as the frame hurtles towards them. The sensation of falling at speed is so strong in my gut that I have to lay my head down and hold it with my hands.

'Alfie!' I'm calling, but he and his big hair are nowhere to be seen. Wherever he is, he can't hear you, my rational brain is telling me. You abandoned the only friend you had in the world. You must face your fate alone.

That's weird; each time I blink the clock has

moved on another hour. I must be drifting in and out of consciousness. My mouth is dry. My temples are throbbing. I need water. An instruction from a wilderness survival book I once read drifts across the haze in front of my eyes: *Do not become dehydrated. Your body will start to shut down.* I must get to the rain container in the grounds.

I'm crawling to the window, feeling my way like a blind beetle, forcing myself through the gap to the outside world. I've done this a hundred times before but today I seem too big for the space. My head is scraping the frame, my arm grazes itself on a small fragment of glass in the wood. My bad leg, which has been well behaved for ages, decides to deliver a spasm of excruciating cramp.

I'm rolling up, clutching my calf muscle. Pain is searing up my leg, across my pelvis and up my spine. I stand, shakily, in an effort to get my blood circulating. I'm half hopping and half leaning against the wall. My sight has narrowed into tunnel vision, which is a sign

that I'm going to pass out. I'm digging my fingernails into my palms to send my brain a different signal, but it's no use. It feels like my fighting spirit is leaving me, seeping out of my pores, trickling from my eye sockets in slow tears.

Survival depends on key factors: Don't panic. Problem solve and find practical solutions. Stay positive.

I can see the text from the manual as if it is on the page. Next to it was a photo of a grizzly bear the writer had escaped from. Amazing that he had time to take a picture.

The slamming of car doors close by snaps into my brain like an electric shock. I feel a jolt through my body and the tunnel widens into normal sight. I'm picking up the vibration of male voices from the wall before my ears detect their low rumbling. Moments later, there is the high-pitched squeal of power tools against metal and wood and a small quake as the front door is prised open.

The men are inside the building. Heavy footsteps

are moving swiftly through the ground floor. They are feet with a mission, laden with intent. They are entering the café and I am clinging to the wall outside, paralysed, like a spider entangled in its own web.

'Get a load of this, George,' says a voice, about two metres from my trembling body.

More footsteps from along the corridor. The flashing of a powerful torch.

'That's what you'd call a des res,' comments a second voice, with irony. 'Look. Window's broke. Probably the way they got in, whoever they are. Not worth sealing it.'

'Nah. No signs of life. Hasn't been used for a bit. Here, George, what do you think of my new scarf?'

'Very nice if you want to look like a satsuma,' comes the reply. 'Take it off. It might have fleas and I don't want them in the van.'

'You check upstairs; I'll do the grounds. Then we're out of here. Place gives me the creeps.'

Move, Caly. Move, now!

I'm across the driveway and into the shrub border like a mouse that has escaped from a trap, dragging its bad leg behind it. I crouch behind a clump of thick, spiky bushes and count to ten, trying to regulate my breathing. One gasp could give me away. One snap of a twig could lead me to the back of that van, an interrogation room and then a cell. And one day there would be a surgeon who'd put a microchip in my brain, turning it to soft scrambled egg, and I could kiss my rule-breaking habits goodbye.

I'm going to stay free. It's not all going to end here, with two bungling security guards.

Shhh, brain; quiet, thoughts. Here comes the wolf to blow your house down. Hear his footsteps, crunch, crunch on the gravel. See his eyes, stark white in the light of the beam that sweeps through the undergrowth. Silence breath, freeze body. Be still, but be ready, in case a rough hand swipes through the thorns to find your neck. Have your claws out and your toes nimble.

He's passing by, the stranger with the dark uniform

and the big boots and radio flashing on his belt. He's turning the corner, checking the perimeter of the building. Following orders, but not looking too closely, in case he doesn't like what he sees.

He's out of sight. The horn of the van is sounding; his partner is getting impatient. Another minute, and there is the slam of a car door and the whine of an engine. The vehicle reverses and turns, then drives slowly away towards the griffins on their pillars. If I had magic powers, I would let them roar and leap and send the intruders away screaming with a fear that would haunt their dreams forever.

I make my way carefully to the rain containers, a mixture of plant pots and buckets, positioned under a broken gutter, and choose the largest, fullest one. I realise I'm shivering. Every joint is aching. Relief or virus? Either way, I need to rest, to put this day behind me, to plan what happens next.

I feel weak and listless. Carrying the water is like hauling a cart up a mountain. I should have chosen the

smallest and lightest, but at least this will save having to make the journey twice.

I reach my home, my des res, and light some candles. I look at the water but can't drink – the thought of it makes me shiver even more. I wrap myself in extra jumpers, coats and blankets and wonder if this is what Dair felt, that night of the fire? Was he so cold he panicked? It would be an explanation. I could kill for the warmth of big flames right now. Maybe I'm beginning to understand.

Ker-thud. There is a strange sound coming from outside my front door. *Ker-thud.* There it is again.

'Alfie, is that you?' I whisper. There is no reply and I'm reaching for the knife on the table.

Now there is a scratching noise, followed by a nibbling. My heart sinks – it's probably a rat. I'll need to chase it away and I'm not in a fit state to chase anything. Cautiously, I go to push open my cardboard door, blade poised in case the rodent leaps at my throat and plunges disease-ridden teeth into my skin.

Slowly, slowly the door opens and I squeal as my eyes encounter something larger than a rat, but furry all the same, with long ears and sharp teeth and pink eyes fixed on me with a nervous stare.

'Furball!' I scream, scooping the soft bundle of fluff into my arms and kissing her head about twenty times. 'You're . . .' but my throat won't allow any more words.

Chapter Twenty-seven

'Where've you been, then, bunnykins?' I say to my long-lost friend when my voice returns. I scratch her under the chin, just the way she likes. 'On an adventure, I expect. I was very worried about you, you know.'

I examine her all over and double-check her injured paw. 'This looks good. All healed now. Clever girl.'

Maybe it's a coincidence, but I'm beginning to feel better. The shivers have stopped and my leg is behaving again. I'm so happy to see Furball. As I stroke her ears, she closes her eyes and drifts away into rabbit dreamland, her whiskers twitching sweetly.

We're two of a kind, she and I. We're both refugees, far from home. We are on the run from the authorities. Our families don't know where we are. There is one difference, though; Furball is living under a death

sentence. This thought makes me cradle her even more tightly.

'I promise I will look after you,' I whisper into her floppy ear. 'We'll carry on together.'

I curl up on my bed, pulling the covers over both of us. The tea-light candles are filling the space with a warm glow. It's a bit of an illusion, as I can see my breath each time I exhale.

What's your plan, Paper Clip?

I have to face the fact that, whatever has happened to Alfie, he will never want to speak to me again. Our friendship is over – it's something I will regret for the rest of my life. But he wasn't honest with me and I'm not sure I could trust him again. I feel betrayed and bruised. I would have told him everything, anything, to make his life better.

So I made a mistake. Not the first time. Won't be the last.

There are things I must do for myself now. I must make a decision about my future and it won't include Alfie.

Tomorrow, I will try to solve the puzzle of Little Bird. First of all, I will hunt through the shopping trolleys and parking machines at the supermarket for a loose pound coin and I will use it to call her. I need to know. Are the FISTS waiting for me? Is the net closing in? Her answer will determine whether I can go home or whether I must keep hiding.

I want to hear her voice so much it hurts. I want to know that she is safe, to feel her arms round me and her fingers stroking my hair. I miss hearing her rhythmic chanting in the early morning and the smell of jasmine which lingers in the air after she's bathed.

There are many ways to live the same life. Little Bird and I have been living with one face for the world and another for behind our front door. We have been pretending we are happy. But it has been like walking on broken glass and not crying out with the pain.

This is what I want to say to her, that we can choose to live another way. And maybe, when the ban on foreign travel is lifted, we can go to her country,

where jacana birds glide over turquoise seas and the beaches are fringed with coconut palms. And where there is a family that will love us both.

If I could fly, Little Bird, I would take us there.

'You can come with us, Furball. I won't leave you behind,' I tell her. My eyelids are as droopy as a bough laden with fat mangoes. As sleep claims me, I imagine myself lulled gently on a warm wave in the Andaman Sea. Pelicans fly overhead and macaque monkeys chatter in the trees.

Chapter Twenty-eight

BANG, BANG, BOOM! My eyes are open. My body is rigid. My heart is racing. I am holding my breath, fearing the world has been blown apart. My brain is trying to tell me I am in my house of books. I can feel Furball still nestled into the curve of my belly. But something is very wrong. There are voices. Vehicles. I can hear the rumble of heavy machinery very close.

And now there is another *BOOM*, louder than the first, a roar that shakes everything from my shelves and my table with a clatter. Glasses and mugs smash on the ground. In an instant, there is chaos, and the air around me is filled with dust and the sound of an enormous engine, revving, reversing, repositioning.

I'm not thinking clearly. My thoughts are paralysed. I'm sitting still amongst debris, while the earth beneath

me trembles. I think this must be shock. I don't know what to do.

BOOM, BOOM, CRASH! Another strike and, with it, the terrible groan of splitting timbers and falling masonry. A rush of dust so thick I am choking and my eyes are full of grit. It's enough to flick my action switch. Instinctively, I reach for a tea towel and tie it around my face, protecting my nose. Then I wrap Furball in a blanket. She doesn't struggle – brave bunny.

We've got to get out of here, but leaving with nothing could be a death sentence – so I try to make a mental list of essentials for survival. I am scrabbling through my drawer, grabbing the knife, my torch and the packet of batteries which have been thrown to the ground. I shove it all in my grubby cotton bag. I fold the plastic sheet which has lain under my bedding into a tight roll and secure it with string.

I'm looking at my clothes and thinking about the weeks of painstaking effort it has taken to assemble a

collection, from skips, from bins, from the porches of charity shops. But I can only take what I can carry.

BOOM, BANG, CRASH! Oh no. Please no. Time is running out. My walls are caving in. Books are falling in slow motion like shrapnel after an aerial attack. There is no sound. I've gone deaf. My mouth feels solid with dirt. I'm shielding Furball from the collapsing structure, my back taking the brunt of the blows from the heavy cookery and wildlife books I used to stabilise the roof struts.

'*Om mani padme hum, om mani padme hum*,' I chant, although my voice is so constricted it is just a whisper. I can see my mother's face with its sweet smile, and there is jasmine and the ting-ting of prayer bells and she is sitting in the courtyard of a golden temple, surrounded by gentle, shaven-headed monks in orange robes.

I am closing my eyes, letting panic overwhelm me with a floating sensation and comforting images in beautiful colours. I feel so sleepy. I could just lie down completely, and bask in the warm, iridescent glow

from the temple roof. The monks are chanting in my head, the rhythm of their words becoming stronger and more insistent.

There is shouting. I'm not sure if it's coming from close by or this surreal place in my imagination. It is a man's voice – one that is familiar. The smile has gone from Little Bird's face and the monks have ceased their prayers. Everyone is staring at the figure emerging from the shadows of the temple, walking towards my mother. The man is of medium height and has a lean, wiry build. He wears jeans, a black T-shirt and trainers. He has short brown hair, balding on top, and on his upper arms there are tattoos of lions. His body is stiff and his movements watchful, braced for a fight. In his left hand, he carries a knife. Its blade is glinting in the fierce sunlight.

I force myself to look at him and I'm instantly filled with a mixture of nausea and fear. The man is moving closer to Little Bird, who has bowed her head and her upper body, in submission. I am straining for clarity

through the sun-haze. The monks become the orange walls of our kitchen; the temple is a photo, in a gold frame. My mind is taking me back home.

'I told you to *come here*,' my father is saying to my mother quietly, menacingly. 'Did you hear me, woman?'

She doesn't reply or move a muscle. She is too terrified.

'Get away from her, Ven, you promised,' I am warning him. I can't bring myself to call him Dad. 'You're drunk.'

'What's this?' he sneers. 'Another little creature with no respect and nothing better to do than tweet. Another one that needs its wings clipped.'

'We are sick of you bullying us. I'm calling the police and it's going to stop,' I tell him, and I'm reaching for the handset. He grabs my arm.

'Oh, Calypso, why don't we dance real slow?' he whispers close in my ear, before spinning me roughly away from the worktop. I let out a gasp as my body

slams into a cupboard. He is right in my face when I turn.

'Don't touch her,' Little Bird shrieks, rushing forward to push him away from me. He stumbles and falls against the pine dresser. My mother is helping me up, her fragile arms trembling.

He recovers his balance and turns to stare at us both. 'Tweet, tweet, tweet, you feather-brained parrots. That's what you do, you squawk and do my head in, twenty-four seven.'

Swear to God, there are daggers in his eyes. With his jaw open and set, he takes a wild step forward and lunges at us with the knife. I pull Little Bird out of the way and cross my arms in front of my face, lashing out with my leg hard against his shin, just as the blade comes down. My mother is screaming. There is a thud and a dull ache in my thigh. There is blood on the knife and my dad is letting out an animal cry so close I can smell the whisky on his breath. From behind, there is a flash of yellow as Little Bird hits him with all her

angry might on the side of his head with our heaviest saucepan. He drops to his knees, confused, but still conscious. The knife clatters to the floor and Little Bird takes it in her hands.

'Run, Calypso, run!' she is shrieking. Her voice sounds like the squeal of an anguished gull. But I am hugging her and we are both crying.

I'm crying now, in loud, terrible sobs.

I did as she told me. And my brain wiped the scene from my memory as quickly as a blade slices through flesh. That's why I had to get away. I understand now. But the puzzle isn't complete. I don't know what she did next, only that she is still alive. Where is my no-good father? We are not safe if he is still near us.

Ven for vengeance, for venom, for vendetta.

Is he out there, somewhere, looking for me? I hold Furball even closer while this thought takes shape.

'Run, Calypso, run!' someone is yelling, not far away. I know the voice, but my brain is in freefall. I can't identify it. Maybe it's just an echo of the past.

BOOM, CRASH, SMASH, BANG!

Suddenly, I am blinded in the full glare of white lights, and I am scrabbling over piles of books, Furball still tucked under my arm. It feels like the world is imploding. All around me, bricks and plaster fall like brown hail. Shards of glass are smashing around my face like jagged rain. Thick clouds of debris are swirling and shape-shifting, just as the starlings do over the beach at sunset.

When the dust settles, I am surrounded by daylight and I am staring at a canary yellow machine. It has a square face on the end, and caterpillar tracks for feet. It is as high as two men. It is a demolition robot, working by remote control. And it is inching forward.

'Run, Caly, run!' I hear again, but my legs don't want to move.

'*Om mani padme hum* . . . Is this where it all ends?' I say to Furball.

I'm scanning the space around us, checking for a way out, but there are men in hard hats and overalls

moving about the grounds, a safe distance from the machine and the crumbling building. Any moment now, there will be a yell because we've been spotted – a kid and a rabbit, who'd have thought? We'll be dragged to safety and there will be questions to answer and I'll be in terrible trouble for leaving my zone, truanting from school, stealing from an ice-cream man, squatting on private land. And being an enemy of the System.

Survivors find practical solutions to their problems. Well, maybe I'm not a survivor after all. Maybe there are no more solutions. I'm telling my feet to move but they are as heavy as lead. This is how it must feel to stand before a firing squad. Luckily, the robot isn't tasked with my destruction.

I'm ready for the moment of discovery. 'This is it, Furball. The end of the line.' I breathe, half scared, half relieved, hoping that when the alarm goes up, the demolition crew will be kind.

There is a loud whistle and a call of, 'OK, Charlie,

ready to go,' and my brain does a somersault, trying to recompute as the robot lifts its neck and stares at me with its featureless face. Am I so camouflaged in dirt, so good at blending with my surroundings, that they can't see me? I'm yelling and waving my free arm but the machine's caterpillar tracks are jolting into motion and the noise of it is obliterating everything else.

It is heading straight for me at high speed.

'Calypso!' someone yells, trying to get my attention – but the voice sounds distant, almost inaudible through the grinding acceleration of the robot. Any second now, they will see me. In another moment, the machine will stop abruptly on its winding tracks.

It isn't slowing down at all. Its head is raised high in the air like a dinosaur rearing on hind legs. The noise is making Furball scrabble in my arms. Without thinking, my muscles relax and release her. She jumps to the ground, hopping away over the piles of books and timber. I am crying out but no sound is leaving my mouth.

Why can't I move? *For God's sake, brain, DO SOMETHING!*

My feet start to scrabble sideways up a mountain of bricks but it's too late. The beast is upon me. I hold my breath and close my eyes and wait for the thud of impact and the excruciating pain that must follow as my bones are crushed like dry sticks under a heavy boot.

BOOM, CRASH, BANG! My stomach lurches as I anticipate the moment of collision. My nerves scream. Adrenaline fills my veins with ice. The beast roars and there is a loud explosion in my ears, then a monsoon deluge of masonry that seems to last for several minutes. At last, I open my eyes, expecting to be face to face with my predator and several pairs of shocked eyes.

The robot is behind me. Somehow, by some miracle, it must have missed me. I am standing amongst the ruins of the hospital. There is nothing left.

There is no pain, not even a scratch. Just a weird

sensation that all my body parts have been rearranged. I must be the lucky one in a million; the one that survives against all the odds.

Chapter Twenty-nine

'Sooty?' says a soft voice, near me. My eyes find its owner, and focus on the figure of a kid about my height with very big hair.

'Hey, Alfie.' I am still rigid like a plank. Seeing my best mate makes me start to tremble, from my head to my toes. My chest is still heaving, but I've run out of tears.

'Come on,' he says gently, holding out his hand. I glance over my shoulder at the yellow beast, whose hazard lights are flashing. Its engine is still turning over, but it is motionless, its head lowered. 'How's your leg?' Alfie asks.

This seems a really stupid question. I've just had a whole three-storey building fall around my head, nearly been run over by a demolition demon and all

Alfie wants to know about is my leg. Now I'm thinking about it, it's sore. But it would be, wouldn't it?

'It hurts,' I say, irritated.

'Good.' Alfie seems relieved. He is still motioning for me to take his hand. 'There's still time.'

'Time for what, Alfie?'

He looks awkward, like there's something he really wants to say but can't find the words.

'Let's get out of here.' He clasps my hand. As his fingers wrap round mine, I feel some strength returning and I try some shaky steps. 'No rush,' he soothes. I'm looking at the men in hard hats, who are busy moving around the site, concerned only with the task of clearing the area. They are taking no notice of us and I don't know whether to be puzzled, angry or relieved. Despite my efforts, I'm going nowhere fast.

'Sit here for a minute,' suggests Alfie, lowering me on to the wooden bench, which has escaped the attention of the robots.

'You got back, then?' I say at last, when my head

stops feeling like it's floating in jelly.

'Well, I wasn't going to stay in that shed with the chicken poo forever,' he replies, obviously slightly hurt.

I'm taking in the view, which is adding to my confusion. Everything has changed. There is just rubble where the hospital stood. It's like being in a monstrous lunar park. The scale of the devastation is so great, I am lost for words. Out of the corner of my eye, I see something white and brown disappearing in and out of the bushes.

'Furball!' I exclaim, but I'm feeling too weak to get up. Alfie gets on to his hands and knees, reaches into the undergrowth and lifts Furball up, putting her on my lap. She looks unhurt after her ordeal. I bury my face in her fur and breathe in her musty warmth. Then I remember the events my memory replayed a few short minutes ago. My chest starts to convulse, my throat tightens and a river of tears begins to pour from my eyes in an unstoppable flow.

Alfie puts an arm round me and holds me tight.

'Everything's going to be all right. Promise.'

'Don't,' I tell him. 'Can't trust promises. Can't trust anyone. I know why my leg is hurting. I remembered. It's so horrible.' I press myself deeper into Furball's softness. 'I just want to go to sleep.' The torrent is subsiding.

'We need to leave,' says Alfie, suddenly standing up, a trace of urgency in his voice. He has both his hands on my shoulders and is gently shaking me back to consciousness. In the jumble of thoughts and images in my head, I am connecting with the fact that Alfie is bunking off school today. And he's doing it for me.

'Not leaving Furball,' I say.

'You don't have to,' he assures me, pulling me up on to my feet.

'Where are we going?' I ask feebly.

'Anywhere. As long as you keep moving.'

Chapter Thirty

Alfie is frog-marching me along the pavement, his arm through mine. He is almost taking my full weight. I am carrying Furball and half walking, half stumbling, trying to keep pace with this boy who seems to have lost his marbles. He has a manic look of determination on his face. We're heading away from the hospital on a road that runs parallel with the coast. From here, there is a 360-degree view. To the south, on a flat, grey sea, there's a long cargo boat with a gunship escort. I know that all the carriers bringing food from Europe have to have protection now because of the risk of hijack. At any other time, I would be excited to see this – I've only ever watched it on the news before. But right now I'm not concerned about the dwindling state of our national supplies. I am staring north, in the direction of home.

'What did you mean, there's still time?' I ask, when we pause for Alfie to retie the laces on his stupid trainers.

'There are some things you need to know,' he answers.

'What things?' I'm losing patience.

'Not here, Caly. Just another few minutes.' His cheeks are flushed bright red from bending down.

'No, Alfie,' I snap, tugging my arm away from his. 'I don't want to play this game any more. Just tell me this Big Thing, whatever it is, and get it over with.'

'Aargggh,' he shouts in frustration, running his hands through his hair. 'You are really stubborn. I'm trying to make it as easy as I can for you. I've never had this trouble before.'

'You've got five seconds, then I'm walking away and you will never see me again.' My voice is low as I try to control my anger.

'You are nearly in the same club as me,' he begins.

'Time's up,' I tell him.

'That's not fair. I didn't hear you counting!'

'I didn't hear you saying anything interesting. Bye, Alfie,' I say, turning and striding, as fast as I can in my state, away from him.

'Right, then,' he calls after me. I imagine he is almost stamping his foot at me.

'Yeah, whatever.' I keep walking, without glancing back.

'Calypso?' he shouts. There is something in his voice that makes me look round. Alfie is standing in the middle of the road. He is facing me. Behind him, there is a mini-bus full of school kids, driving at full speed. It's gaining on him fast. This is a stupid stunt to get my attention. Clearly, Alfie has lost not just his marbles but his sense of self-preservation.

'ALFIE! Get out of the road! Are you barking up a fruit and nut tree?' He doesn't move, just stares at me. The mini-bus doesn't even brake. Honest to God, it drives through him and continues along the road, past where I am standing with my mouth open. The

children ignore me, apart from a girl with plaits sitting at the back, who sticks out her tongue.

Alfie shoves his hands in his baggy jean pockets and starts to walk towards me. When he is standing in front of me, he reaches out and, with the tip of a finger, pushes my jaw up into a closed position.

'Like I was saying, Sooty, it's a weird club, but there are some good things about it. No exams. No school, actually, unless you feel like it. No wrinkles. No getting old. No pain. You can always be a kid. Everywhere is a playground. And friends can last forever, not just a lifetime.' Alfie puffs out his cheeks with a big sigh, as if a burden has lifted.

'The robot . . .' I begin. 'Oh my God. It didn't drive round me, did it?'

Alfie shakes his head. He is too slow to catch me as I sit down on the pavement with a bang, my muscles incapable of holding me up. Furball hops free and begins to investigate the sparse winter grass on the verge.

'Freakin' Friday,' I say quietly.

'The thing is . . . you're not *quite* in the club yet. You have to decide,' says Alfie, kicking a twig with his foot, not making eye contact.

'I don't understand,' I tell him.

'The pain in your leg. It means you're still connected.'

'Trains are connected, Alfie, sausages are connected. What am I connected to?'

'To your self,' he answers. 'There's still time to go back, maybe. That's what I meant when I said you're *nearly* one of the club.'

I swallow hard. Is Alfie telling me that I am 'almost' dead? That somewhere my whole self is existing without this bit of me? That I've been leading a parallel life – and that the mate I've been counting on isn't even alive?

It's too much to take in. Any minute now, I'm hoping Alfie's face will crack up and he'll say, 'Gotcha, Sooty,' and do a little victory dance. In fact, I'm holding my breath, waiting for it – but nothing comes.

'How long ago did you . . .?' I ask, at last.

'Three years. Pneumonia. Died in the hospital. Became a Watcher. I look out for kids after they've, well, you know.'

No, no, NOOOOO. I'm shaking my head. I don't believe I'm talking to a dead guy. Freakin' Friday doesn't cover it. All the other days of the week are in there too.

'Sorry,' I manage to say. Poor Alfie. Poor Alfie's mum, who lost her whole family. No wonder she works nights and all the hours she can. No wonder Alfie comes and goes as he pleases. No wonder he was so lost and lonely when I met him. There is a silence between us. Alfie is allowing me time to come to terms with my situation.

'I don't get it. Some people can see me,' I tell him. 'There was a kid on that bus just now. And in a front garden. A woman in the launderette. And Dair . . . They can't all be –'

'Brown bread.' Alfie nods. I turn quickly to look at

Furball. I raise my shoulders in a question and Alfie just smiles in answer.

'No!' I exclaim and move to the rabbit, scooping her up for a cuddle. 'It's not true, is it, Furball? None of it.'

'You only lose all your substance right at the end. That's why it was dangerous for a bit because your essence is visible.' Alfie is speaking slowly, or maybe my mind isn't processing the words at the usual speed. 'You're fading all the time, though, so after a while you become invisible to the eye. But it's still dodgy. There are people who've been between life and death who can sometimes see others who've entered that state. Mums can often see or sense the presence of a child too. That's why I couldn't ask you over. I really wanted to.'

'Jeez, Alfie, all that running from the police. It was for nothing,' I say, resentment bubbling under the surface of my voice.

'I think the beach cop saw you in the boat. But,

anyway, I had to try to keep it real for you until you remembered how you got your injury. You have to know, before you can decide. That's how it works. I don't make the rules.'

'Well, who does?' I ask.

'Dunno. They get passed down from the Watchers to the Arrivals. Then the Arrivals become Watchers, and so it goes on.' He's looking at me intently.

'So you've helped lots of kids?' I ask.

'Yeah,' says Alfie with a grin. 'Like I said, you're the most trouble. But at least you're halfway sensible. Some of them have never even tied their laces themselves, let alone had to survive.'

'So you watch over them while they sort themselves out and, when they're ready to deal with it, you tell them they can go back,' I say.

'Going back isn't always possible. Sometimes, they're full members of the club on arrival. Like Dair.'

'But he was sick. How could that happen?' My brain feels like it's frying, trying to make sense of everything.

'You come as you are, with all your good bits and your bad bits – problems, worries, bad habits, issues. Dair was a one-off. He tried to resist everything. His illness wasn't real.'

'It looked real to me,' I say, overwhelmed with sadness for Dair.

'His mind recreated symptoms from his past,' explains Alfie. 'It wasn't safe for you to be with him any longer. He liked playing with fire. Always did. That's why he arrived in the first place. That's why he had to be moved on.'

'What do you mean?'

'He was your first Watcher, Caly. But his mind was messed up. He was supposed to look out for you. It ended up being the other way round.' Alfie is trying to keep an edge out of his voice.

'They did it to him,' I say quietly. 'He started out like me, a kid who broke the rules. But they put a chip in his brain.'

'That's why you were put together, because of your

similarities. But he never really accepted that he was dead. He thought he was still a freedom fighter. And he would never let himself get caught.'

'So he started the fire because I went for help?' The penny is beginning to drop, as Gran would say. 'Where is he now?'

Alfie shrugs. 'Somewhere else, nowhere. He was moved on. I don't know what that means.'

There is silence between us for a few moments. I'm hoping Dair is happy where he has gone and that his mind is at peace. And then I remember I have a choice to make and that there may be a life line. 'You said there might be time for me.'

Alfie nods, kicks the twig again and hunches his shoulders. 'Yeah. You get to decide.'

'And every minute counts?' I ask. Alfie nods. 'So if we'd waited much longer to have this conversation, it might have been too late?'

'I wanted to tell you somewhere nice and peaceful so that you could weigh it all up,' he replies defensively.

'I tried, that night of the fair. But your mind wasn't ready. You hadn't remembered enough. And you got in a strop.' Alfie pulls a face.

'So where were you taking me?' I ask.

'A playground about five minutes away. That's where my Watcher took me.'

'Sounds nice,' I say, slipping my arm through his, standing close to him. I suddenly don't feel in a hurry at all.

'It's a big decision, Caly. If you go back, you have to face up to everything you ran away from – not just your injury.'

'But I'll have you to watch over me, right?' I have a strange sensation in my heart. It feels like it's being wrenched in two.

Alfie is shaking his head slowly. 'You'll lose contact with me and Furball. You'll probably have no memory of your time with us.' He sounds so sad.

'But you can ride scooters and collect treasure and throw filibusters and everything, so you could hang

around if you wanted to. That wouldn't be bending the rules, would it?' I ask.

Alfie looks downcast. 'The connection will end. I'm not allowed any contact with Arrivals who have gone back,' he says quietly.

'I don't think much of that rule, then,' I tell him.

He smiles at me, then thrusts his hands in his pockets. My mind is racing, throwing up questions.

'What's it to be, then?' Alfie asks hesitantly.

'Ask me when we're on top of the world.'

Chapter Thirty-one

'Come on,' calls Alfie. 'What kept you?'

He's sitting on the platform of a big red slide. I'm not sure where his burst of energy came from. He took off like a rocket as soon as the playground came into view. I saw him jump the wire fence with my own eyes. Crease would give him a high five for that.

This place has been built at the end of a dead-end street that opens up unexpectedly on to a wide green. There are ten different climbing frames, two slides, four swings and a sand pit with a soft tarmac strip, suitable for long-jump. The red slide is the highest point in the town. From this angle, Alfie's hair seems to scrape the sky.

I'm rattling the locked metal gate like a toddler in a cot. Since when did they start banning kids from using

the equipment on a weekday? Furball is looking at me quizzically. The clanking noise is making her whiskers twitch. There's nothing for it but to follow Alfie's lead and do a drop swing manoeuvre, if my leg will let me. I'm willing it to hurt more, which is one of the weirdest wishes to make.

I propel myself over the top, landing as lightly as a jacana bird, and in less than thirty seconds I'm climbing the steps and joining Alfie on the red grid. There is just room for two and we sit in silence, hugging our knees in the cold breeze, looking out over the northern horizon to the edges of the town and the big swathe of countryside that separates it from my home zone.

I lean against Alfie slightly. He doesn't change his gaze; he seems lost in thought. We are both aware that the clock is ticking and that the next hour will change our existences forever.

'So where am I really?' I ask at last. Of the dozens of questions gnawing at my mind, this is the most

pressing. I feel I need to understand the whole picture, if my brain can take it in.

'You are here,' responds Alfie simply. 'This isn't a dream.'

'But I've left my self behind. You mean my body?'

'You're probably in hospital. That's what usually happens.'

'So I could have been there for weeks.'

Alfie shakes his head. 'Separation doesn't work in real time. You could have been in hospital just a few days,' he explains. I look mystified. 'You can be in two places at once, and so can time.' Now I'm lost, completely and utterly. 'Sorry, Sooty. I'm no good at this bit. You need a degree in quantum mechanics to get it properly.'

I rub my head with my hands. These facts are orbiting my brain like out-of-control planets. I try to picture myself in our local hospital, flat out, with monitoring equipment bleeping to register my breathing. I imagine Little Bird sitting by me, chanting

quietly for my recovery. Is Ven there too, a dark shadow pacing in the background, or was he arrested at the scene? If I was found outside, away from the house, he could have hidden the knife and told the authorities a bunch of lies about me being attacked. Would Little Bird have been strong enough to tell the truth, knowing that her life was in danger?

I'm shivering and it's not with the cold. Alfie is looking at me with a concerned expression.

'My dad,' I say simply. He just nods – he must have guessed what happened. There are probably only so many situations that bring kids to this new world: accidents, illness and violence, either self-inflicted or suffered.

'You could move in, like I said.' He sounds so hopeful.

'And share your map posters?' I dig him playfully in the ribs.

'And my explorer's books,' he says.

'Hmmm. Tempting.' I pull a face. He looks a bit

hurt, so I put my hand on his knee. 'What would you do, if you were me? Don't tell me you're not allowed to answer that.'

'I don't know what you've left behind, whether there's enough good stuff to go back for. Growing up's pretty hard, so they say.' He smiles. 'But you could have a great life: travelling the world, having a dozen kids, being a film star, or a lion tamer, driving a pink sports car, running for president. Whatever you want, you could make it happen. And you'd have lots of years with your mum. And all the great things you achieve would make her really proud. I wish I could have done that for my mum.'

'If I stay, I'd have you,' I say. Alfie nods.

'Bit of a no-brainer,' he says. 'A best mate for eternity and a rabbit that never needs cleaning out. You could be a Watcher too – we could work together. Partners.'

I consider this, picturing what my future would hold: endless games and adventures; freedom to move

anywhere and everywhere; a different kind of life, with no risk of disease or pain and no chance of looking like my wrinkly gran with her wispy, white hair, saggy tights and missing teeth.

My fingers close round something hard in my pocket. It's the metal bottle top. I take it out and look at it.

'What's that?' asks Alfie.

'Dair gave it to me. He thought it was the key to the Hive. He wanted me to promise I would carry on fighting the System. So you were right, Alfie. Dair and I are alike. There are things I want to fight for too. I want to build a new life for me and Mum. I want to show Ven he hasn't destroyed me. And people should know what they do to kids in the detention centre. There have to be changes. Maybe it's up to me to start making them. So I think what I'm saying is I need to have that chance, Alfie. I have to go back.'

Alfie puffs his cheeks out, as if the words are a body blow. 'All because of a bottle top some crazy guy gave you?'

'No. Because of my mum and Crease and the Feathers. And because of you. I wouldn't have made it this far without you.' I let my head rest on my knees so that I can't see Alfie's sad expression.

'It'll be dangerous,' he says. 'You could end up like Dair.'

I look at Alfie. I don't feel quite so brave any more. He reads my expression.

'You don't feel sleepy or anything, do you?' Alfie is poking my arm. 'You're very quiet.'

'Wide awake,' I confirm.

'Don't decide yet. I've thought of something. A bit like flipping a coin,' he says. 'Come on.'

Alfie doesn't wait for my reply. He is already hurtling down the slide, jumping off the end and running to the swings. I want to point out to him that my entire future can't be decided by something as mad as a game of heads and tails. It's a silly idea.

I lie on my belly and slip down after him. By the time I reach the swings, Alfie is like a pendulum in

motion, rising higher and higher.

'It's easy,' he says, legs extending and folding in a rhythm. 'We both go as high as we can and if you're the first to loop the loop, you stay, if not, you go.'

'You know I'll want to be the first,' I point out, excited by the challenge. 'Which is a clever way of making sure I stay.'

'Not just clever. Genius,' says Alfie with a grin.

'I'm not promising.' I sit on the black rubber seat, taking hold of the chains either side and pushing off the ground with my feet. It feels great to be in the air, the momentum increasing with each swing. Our legs work in synchronicity and very soon, at the top of each curve, we are level with the bar. It won't take much more effort to send the seats into a 360-degree loop. Alfie is laughing like a lunatic and, despite everything, I'm giggling too, feeling the rush of wind through my hair, the coldness making my teeth tingle. I'm not thinking about The Decision, or that this might be the last time I get to go wild with Alfie. I'm not weighing

up the benefits of being an eternal child. With each swoop, I'm ascending higher and higher. Soaring like an eagle. I have never felt so exhilarated, happy or free.

'Stand up,' he says, nimbly tucking his feet under his body and pulling up whilst in motion. I copy him, with more difficulty. It seems to make us move even faster.

'Ready?' says Alfie as we travel in reverse. We seem to pause for a nanosecond, suspended in the sky. I give him the thumbs up sign with one hand.

'*WAAY!*' we both yell as the two swings start to drop. They curve and ascend together, but this time, there is no judder as they start to falter. Both of us are moving in a complete arc and in a moment we are above the bar, upside down, staring at the ground. Our stomachs lurch, our bodies brace, our lips drop and leave our teeth exposed like white horseshoes. A split second later, we are descending again, hands and feet braced in a star position. We allow the swings to lose momentum and come to a gradual stop.

Furball hops over to us and stands on her hind legs,

her nose twitching at both of us in turn. I jump off the swing and pick her up for a cuddle. She nestles softly into my neck for a moment, allowing me to stroke the side of her belly. But then her back legs begin to scrabble against me impatiently and her throat makes a strange, growling noise.

'Hey, what's up?' I ask her. She continues to brace against my hold so I put her down, very gently. She runs a few paces, then looks behind at me. Her tail is moving from side to side like a mini windscreen wiper.

'She's telling me something,' I say to Alfie. 'What is it?'

'Just rabbiting on, as usual,' he replies.

Suddenly, she takes off at full speed, runs out of the playground, through the fence and into the undergrowth. Flashes of brown and white tell me she's sniffing about under the bushes, on her own little mission.

And, watching her, I realise several things: that my thoughts are clear (it must be the rush of blood to my

head), that my choice has been made and that my leg is hardly hurting at all.

There's one other thing I'm aware of. Alfie has turned away from me and is rubbing his eyes with his sleeve.

Chapter Thirty-two

It feels like flying. We are flamingos, treading water with wide strides, about to take off. Our feet are barely touching the ground. I am following Alfie's lead, a few paces behind, along pavements, across roads, past shops and churches and through parks. Where cars are parked in our path, we are leaping over them. It is almost effortless. My body seems weightless, my joints as flexible as rubber. There is no friction, no pain, no fear.

This is free running, Crease, but not as you've ever imagined in your wildest dreams.

Alfie says it's best for me to avoid blending with objects as it can hasten disconnection from my 'real' body, so I am learning the art of 'spiriting' – travelling at speed over the terrain as lightly as a summer breeze.

The only sensation is one of air shifting as I move through it. And the *thump-thumping* of my heart, so loud it seems it wants to burst out of my chest. I have begun a race, but there are no other competitors. There is a finish line, but I may reach it too late. I am here and I am there. There are forces pulling me in both directions but the forward momentum is the stronger. We are moving north and have already lost the smell of the sea.

I am kannika seed, carried on the wind.

I am steam from a mangrove swamp, swirling along the forest floor.

I am Calypso, rising.

Little children are spilling from a school ahead of us, carrying rolls of art-work under their short arms, felt-tipped fingers clasped around lunch-boxes and papier-mâché models of angels. Some wear wings made of wire and netting and have tinsel haloes on their heads. They sound like a family of macaques, each trying to screech louder than the other.

Alfie and I weave round them, over them, and feel the buzz of collective energy, like a force field. A lollipop man waits patiently in the middle of the street for a wriggling blue and black centipede to cross in front of him. Alfie can't resist flicking his yellow lollipop and making it spin as we pass. The poor man looks accusingly at the children and then all around in confusion.

I catch up with Alfie and waggle my finger at him. He just shrugs and grins, but the moment of fun is soon forgotten as we press on with our journey. I sense the urgency building with every minute that passes.

Everything feels as if it is moving past us in fast-forward mode. There are glimpses of fairy lights in house windows, a Union Jack flying from a mast, an oversized reindeer waving a hoof from the step of a convenience store.

We have reached the most northern part of the town, where the tarmac and ordered grid of houses end and the wide fields begin. Some still have maize and

barley crops lying flat and black. There was no proper harvest because of the virus. It looks as if every acre has been sprayed with chemicals. One rectangular field has an untidy pile of straw bales at one end, stacked unevenly, their plastic casings ripped and flapping.

There is no sign of livestock anywhere. Beyond the orange mesh security fence, I count at least three tractors, abandoned on the edges of half-ploughed fields. The landscape looks heavy and sad. In the far distance are the downlands, and I feel myself shiver. On the other side of their gentle green slopes is my home zone: my house, my mother, my father, the situation I left behind, and my worst nightmare.

'Are we going the right way?' asks Alfie, sensing my unease. I nod without making eye contact. He reaches across for my hand, which he squeezes tightly. His feels cool, despite our exertions.

We are looking down on the motorway which weaves away from the town and runs from here all

the way to the Scottish border, like the spine of the country. There are still restrictions on journeys out of, or into, different zones. The four lanes look eerily empty – just the occasional white van, lorry or official-looking car is passing along slowly, observing the speed limit imposed last year to save fuel.

I recognise this place. We are near the car park where Mr Carter, the ice-cream man, unwittingly took me on board. There is no sign of his van today, nor of any other visitors. The gate across the entrance has a sign on it which reads *Keep Out. Infection Zone.* There is rust on the chain securing the gate to its post. It hasn't been opened for a long time. The thick metal links won't keep us out, I'm thinking. We can't be locked in, restricted, controlled. But where I'm going there are different kinds of chains. I can almost feel their weight as I imagine them coiling round me.

'Wait,' I say to Alfie. There are sudden, violent tremors vibrating through my body. I gasp in anxiety. 'What's happening to me?'

'Sooty, this is all new. I've never helped anyone go back before,' Alfie replies. He looks wide-eyed and frightened.

'You don't have to come.' I'm hugging myself to disguise the shaking. 'I can retrace my steps from here.' I'm putting on a brave face, but the thought of never seeing Alfie again is making white-hot flames burn my heart.

'I know it's stupid –' he shrugs – 'but I've never left the zone before. Just what you need – a guardian angel with agoraphobia.'

'Hey. You'll be fine,' I try to reassure him. 'And, whatever happens, so will I.' At this moment, I don't believe it. But Alfie sighs and holds out his hand to give me a high five. Mine meets his and they stay clasped for several seconds. With our hands touching, I can't imagine life any other way. As I make myself release my fingers, I notice the energy between us. It seems to say that together we are strong – and that makes what I am about to do even harder.

'We should head for the hospital in your zone – that's the most likely place you'll be,' Alfie says.

'They don't take kids there.' I remember now. 'That's why I was sent to our hospital for treatment before.'

'But with your injury, you'd be an emergency. Think, Caly. Where is it? It's really important.'

I'm shaking my head. My mind's a blank.

'They're always named after kings or queens or presidents, or things like faith, hope, religious people . . .' Alfie is racking his brains.

Then it hits me. 'St Francis. That's what my mum said in the garden. "Take care of my child, St Francis." I thought she'd switched faiths or something. But it's the name of the Accident and Emergency hospital. That's it, Alfie. That's where I am.'

We exchange a glance. 'Right, then,' he says.

'Alfie?' I look at him. He looks back, hopefully. 'Laces.' I point at his trainers, which are almost completely undone. Before Alfie can react, I bend

down and tie them both really tight. 'Double knots,'
I tell him. 'Or you'll go bum over bonce.'

'Nag, nag.' He shrugs, with quite a big sniff.

Chapter Thirty-three

'We have to speed up,' warns Alfie, grabbing my hand and pulling me down the slope that falls away steeply from the car park. We aren't keeping to the mud-smeared footpath, but descending the steepest part of the hill. The tufts of tall grass and clumps of thorny bushes don't slow our pace. We're in the air more than on the ground, each step launching us forward like Olympic long-jumpers.

'*Waay!*' I can't help exclaiming, as we leap a stile in a high wire fence and land several metres beneath on a spiky carpet of straw.

A lazy winter sun, low in the sky, is staring at us through its wide, unblinking eye. I'm running to catch my own shadow, which is as faint as smoked glass.

Across acres turned to mud, over hedges and a

swollen stream, full of dead, floating fish, past the tree with roots like a fat man's legs, around the deep wood, along the road to nowhere, through a recreation ground, under the barrier on the edge of town, back into my home zone – the journey that first took me more than a day has been completed in minutes. I feel breathless with the shock of it.

Alfie and I stand for a moment, getting our bearings. The observation tower lies due north. There's the trading estate to our right with its large, grey warehouses and small roads connecting them. We should navigate our way through them to the centre of town. But my tremors are getting worse and I'm shaking from head to foot.

'Will you wait for me?' I ask Alfie. It's a massive ask, but I need to know the answer. 'When I die properly, we can be together always.'

'I don't know how long I'll be a Watcher,' he replies. 'We all seem to disappear in the end.'

'Where do you think you'll go?' It's hard to keep

the panic out of my voice.

'Dunno.' He shrugs. 'Like I said, I don't make the rules.'

Alfie is holding my gaze. He can read the confusion in my face, the wavering of my heart. I am the one with choices, after all. If I stay, he and I could travel the world. His maps could be the start of real adventures – scaling mountains, crossing deserts, exploring jungles. We could run across oceans, hitching rides on the backs of whales. We could stand on the crown of the Statue of Liberty in New York. We could dance in the Palace of the Winds in Jaipur and sail down the Zambezi river on the snouts of hippos. In Thailand, I could race him to the top of tall coconut trees and chase him between the wooden boats in the floating markets like a mischievous sea monkey. And in the royal palace we could sit on the giant golden Buddha's broad shoulders, smiling at tourists.

We could play forever, laugh forever, exist forever the way we are now. But something stronger is drawing

me back, reeling me in, like a fish on a hook. I want to be complete. I want to be able to speak to Little Bird. I want to feel her love – I want to finish growing up. I want to survive.

'It's this way, I think.' I take Alfie's hand and we skirt swiftly along the side of the massive buildings. A rush of air is rattling the structures, making an eerie *woo woo* sound as we pass. Is it icy cold? I have no way of knowing. I can only feel its force.

The industrial estate merges into a large housing grid and this leads to a main road. We follow it past a superstore, a football stadium, a sixth-form college. On the traffic signs, there is a red Accident and Emergency sign pointing ahead. My shakes have not subsided and are now slowing us down. Alfie takes matters into his own hands, plonking me on the back of a motorbike waiting at traffic lights. He perches behind, wedging me between the rider, a middle-aged man in leather trousers, jacket and helmet, and himself. The square box fixed above the bike's rear

wheel reads *Pappa Pietro's Pizza Emporium.*

'He could be going anywhere,' I say over my shoulder. I'm grateful to have the chance to rest, though.

'We'll jump off as soon as we get near the town centre.'

When the lights go green, the bike accelerates away and begins to weave in and out of the traffic. It's good that this stranger can't feel my hands tightly gripping his waist – at least I hope he can't. Alfie has his arms round my middle, luckily, as I'm starting to sway with a strange, dizzy sensation.

We've entered a one-way system, which snakes round the centre of town. I recognise where we are now. CCTV cameras mounted on aerial pedestrian walkways are tracking our progress. The traffic signs confirm that we are still travelling in the right direction for the hospital. But our driver has other plans, it seems, as he is indicating right and moving towards the centre lane. When he stops in a queue, Alfie yells at me to jump off.

'Phew,' he says. 'That was close.'

We're standing on the pavement and the motorbike is speeding out of sight. I don't remember how we got here. My mind is full of bright, white light, which is making me squint.

'Can't be far now. Lean on me,' Alfie says, putting my arm round his shoulders. We set off again on foot, moving faster than the cars next to us, covering a lot of ground with each stride.

We travel down an underpass where the air is thick with heavy fumes and the engines drone like giant bees. Red monster eyes blink at us in the dark. As we pass them, I see they are the rear lights of vehicles, ascending towards the daylight. We reach the exit and are blinded by sunshine.

My head is spinning. The red dots that have imprinted themselves on my vision are replaced by the intermittent flash of silver blue. There's the *whoop whoop* of a slow siren and the sound of doors slamming. Alfie pulls me back as a person on a stretcher is carried

just in front of us towards sliding glass doors.

'Are we here, Alfie?' I ask, but he doesn't answer. He is watching the security guards who are standing either side of the entrance, their sub-machine guns held at hip height. At least here there are no crowds fighting for anti-viral drugs.

Alfie motions for me to follow him. We stay close to the man and woman in paramedic overalls and enter a wide area with a shiny floor. It's like a hotel foyer, with staff in surgical masks seated behind a long desk beneath an electronic notice board. *Please report to the reception desk. There is a 30 minute wait,* it reads. *If you think you have the H2Z1 virus, please exit the building immediately and proceed to the clinic at our West Street entrance.*

We head towards swing doors marked *Assessment Ward*, seizing the moment a nurse pushes them open to slip through. There are several large rooms leading from an open area and each has at least ten occupied beds. Alfie props me against a wall and makes a quick tour of the area, merging through drawn curtains,

reappearing with a glum look on his face.

'You're not here,' he tells me, taking my hand and whisking me back to the main reception. He is scanning the lists of departments on the board, muttering their names as he does so.

'Cardiac, Geriatric, Neurology, Gynaecology, Urology, Surgical, Intensive Care . . . Second floor . . . Come on!'

We're climbing stairs in big leaps. Alfie is practically lifting me, although his feet are barely touching the ground.

Another armed security guard stands on patrol at the entrance to the second floor. He is chewing gum with his mouth open and watching the hallway. His eyes move left and right like a pendulum. We pass by him undetected and are moving quickly down a long corridor, past wards and busy waiting areas. I feel like a passenger on a platform, watching train windows speed by, the faces behind them just a blur. My brain is confused. I am the one in motion.

'Hey!' shouts a distressed man, sitting with his back against a wall. 'Hey, you!'

'Don't look back,' says Alfie, increasing our pace.

'Can he see us?' I ask, bemused and a little fearful.

'There'll be a lot here who can. We can't get involved.'

The man's voice rings in my ears. 'I don't feel so well, Alfie,' I say feebly. I'm not sure if he's heard me. He keeps repeating 'ICU' over and over again. We make a sharp right turn and are faced with another reception desk. A male nurse is talking quietly to two policemen. The patients in this area are silent. The only noise is made by machines, delivering fluids and oxygen and monitoring breathing. Relatives sit by bedsides, looking hopeful, afraid or exhausted.

My body almost snaps with a sudden force, making me stumble. 'Alfie?' I whisper, reaching for him. He eases me down into a chair and holds both my hands.

'I'll find you, Caly, just stay here.' He looks intently into my eyes, then he is gone.

I'm listening to the regular pulse of medical

equipment, to the squeak of rubber soles on the polished floor, to the hushed words being spoken by the desk, to the distant noise of a television, to water splashing against a metal sink, to a phone ringing, to doors flapping shut, to a kettle boiling, to the click of a switch, to the flush of a loo, to a low moan of pain, to the jingle of keys in a pocket, to the rustle of papers, to the slam of a filing cabinet, to the clink of metal instruments being replaced in a dish.

My ears are suddenly as sensitive as satellites.

Looking out at the gulls, high on the slipstream, I feel the air filtering through their feathers and the *throb, throb, throb* of their wings as they change direction and beat against the current. Every sound of every moving creature and object on the planet is bombarding my brain. I put my head in my hands, hoping that oblivion will come quickly.

Beneath the intense sound, there is a rhythm. Slowly, the chaos of noise begins to fade and the beat becomes more distinct. It is drawing me in, like

a lighthouse might a shipwrecked sailor. It is familiar, safe, and I am starting to recognise the repetition, not just as a pulse, but a phrase. The words are becoming clear, like a signpost in the fog.

Om mani padme hum.

My body jolts again. I gasp. My eyes stare wildly around me at the faces of strangers. No one can help me. Nobody here knows I exist. I grip the wooden arms of the chair and force myself to concentrate. I must stay conscious and wait for Alfie. I must continue to hope. I must focus on the rhythm.

Om mani padme hum, om mani padme hum.

I fix my gaze straight ahead, past the desk, to a room along the corridor, with a glass window. There is a female police officer standing outside it. Inside, a dark-haired woman is sitting with her head bowed. Her body is motionless, but even from this distance, I can see her lips moving.

I am walking towards her with unsure steps. I can no longer feel my feet make contact with the floor. The

uniformed officer stares at me, through me. She sniffs and scratches her pretty nose. She checks her watch. She touches her neck as I stand next to her, my face very close to the glass panel, looking in at the hunched figure on the other side, whose delicate face is etched with pain.

My hands lift up to the clear glass and rest against it, merging with it. I want to reach out to her, envelop her. But I can't disturb her fragile peace. Her eyes are closed. She is chanting, praying next to an empty bed. In her hands are my jeans, the same ones I am wearing now, except those she clutches are soaked with dark blood.

'Little Bird, I'm here,' I say.

Chapter Thirty-four

There is a hand on my shoulder and Alfie is here. He takes in the scene before him, the tears streaming down my face, the Thai woman, as small as a doll, bent over in grief. Now he is beckoning with his other hand. No words, just a movement, and I am following him.

We are leaving this area and moving down a different corridor, turning left, turning right, avoiding trolleys stacked with fresh laundry and patients in wheelchairs.

There are double doors ahead and a sign that reads *Theatre 1* over them. Alfie has stopped outside them. He is looking at me intently.

'In here?' I ask tentatively.

He nods and pushes the door ajar. Another set of doors lies ahead and through their rectangles of clear

glass I can see a surgical team working on a patient under bright white lights. A man in green overalls with a mask and cap is bending low over the patient's chest area.

'Stand clear,' he says, and the others take a step back. There is a loud noise from inside the operating room and almost instantaneously, my body jolts for a third time, sending me crashing into the wall, which I instantly merge with. Alfie pulls me back, a terrified look on his face.

'You have to go in there, Caly,' he says, his lip quivering noticeably. I glance back to the surgeon, who is shaking his head and pulling off his mask. The monitor next to the patient is showing a series of flat lines. The rest of the team looks despondent. A nurse is turning off switches one by one.

It has taken me a few seconds to understand all this, the fact that I am the patient on the table and that they have tried three times to resuscitate me. I turn to look at Alfie, who's motioning for me to move forward and

holding his chest to stop it heaving at the same time.

And now I am hugging him, holding him, like I am clinging on to life itself and whispering, 'I will never forget you,' in his ear and planting a soft kiss on his cheek and he is saying, 'Go, just go,' through tears and I am pressing the metal bottle top into his hand, and saying, 'Remember me.' I'm releasing him and moving backwards, keeping eye contact with him until someone behind me opens the doors and the surgeon passes us and I turn and enter the theatre.

I gasp and a rush of oxygen travels down my windpipe and inflates my chest. I'm aware of three things – an ache in my ribs, a strong smell of antiseptic and a babble of surprised voices. My eyes are closed. I want to lie very still. I'm not sure what is real any more. I'm waiting for Alfie to tell me what has happened, but my craving for his voice is unanswered.

I sense a commotion and footsteps and the squeak of something heavy being wheeled aside. There is a

different energy close by. The nerves in my upper body tingle in response to it. Any moment now, my best mate will be saying something to make me smile. It's not his fault we were too late.

A hush has descended. I feel a warmth like angel breath caressing my cheek, the softness of skin against my skin. There is jasmine in the air. My right hand is raised, enfolded in another's, touched by lips. The contact is delicate, like being lifted on a songbird's wing. I feel it in every cell of my body.

I am ready to open my eyes.

Meet Jill Hucklesby

Hi, Jill. Tell us a bit about your childhood and teenage years. Where did you live, and what were your interests?
I was born in Brighton and lived at the top of a hill with my parents, my sister and brothers in a flat with a spooky cellar. You could hear trains passing by in deep tunnels underneath. It made me think there was a subterranean world existing beneath my bed.

Growing up was a bit of a bumpy time involving loss and the arrival of step family. I often escaped into imaginary worlds! I discovered a love for music and drama, and I also learned to sail.

As a teenager, I worked in a sweet shop (bliss!), then at M&S, so life became a blur of school exams, bras and knickers (my department) and dates with a dark-haired student at college ...

Did you have any favourite books or authors?
Yes, I loved stories about animals. *Black Beauty* by Anna Sewell, *Call of the Wild* by Jack London (cried for days), *Tarka the Otter* by Henry Williamson (ditto). Later, I studied English Lit and loved everything by D. H. Lawrence, E.M. Forster and Thomas Hardy, especially *Tess of the D'Urbervilles*. And if we're including dramatists, Will Shakespeare, of course.

Who's your favourite fictional character?
Two favourites: Tess from *Tess of the D'Urbervilles*, who is stalked by tragedy despite her innocence, and Flora Poste from Stella Gibbons' *Cold Comfort Farm*, who hauls her mad, rural

relatives into the twentieth century with cool, common sense. It's one of the funniest books I've read.

In *If I Could Fly*, Caly sometimes longs to go and live in Thailand, and there are some beautiful descriptions of the country. Have you ever been there? Is there anywhere you would especially love to live?
I travelled for several weeks through Thailand a few years ago with my young family, and fell completely in love with the country. The vibrant colours of the temples and night markets have stayed with me, together with the sounds of monkeys chattering in the trees and elephants bathing in the rivers. And I've never seen a sky so full of stars.

I feel very lucky to live by the sea in Sussex, close to wonderful downland walks and four miles from a buzzy, cultural city. I love the open landscape here. It's where my roots are and I can't imagine living anywhere else.

Caly builds a house of books, and collects bits and bobs to make her feel more at home in the hospital. What is your most treasured possession?
Can that be plural? If so, I would say my photo albums. They hold so many memories, especially of my daughter growing up and our adventures with our three rescued retrievers, Luke, Zack and now Henry the hooligan.

When did you first start writing? What did you do before you were a published author?
I wrote poems and stories from an early age and started to do it seriously when I was studying for a degree in English and

Drama. After working in theatre and journalism, I trained as a screenwriter and wrote for children's TV. I also got involved in a musical theatre development group in London. An idea for a TV drama series was then optioned for production and when it didn't go ahead, the producer suggested I write the book instead. So my first novel, *Deeper Than Blue*, started to take shape and was published in 2007. Happily, I am about to write my sixth book!

Where do your ideas come from? What inspired you to write *If I Could Fly*?
Ideas are strange things. They are always tumbling about, probably because there has always been an alternative world going on in my head. Sometimes a title will come first. Or it might just be a feeling, a rhythm, a voice. Or a question – what if? I usually let them float about for a few days to see if they are going to stay. If they do, I write a short outline, to see where the story will go.

If I Could Fly began to form in the spring of 2009. All my previous books have been about teens who have to face big challenges in their lives, but I wanted this new one to have an extra element – a twist. I could hear Caly running in my head, but for a long time I didn't know what she was running from. I liked the unfolding mystery of her situation. Hope readers will too!

Do you have any advice for readers who are hoping to follow in your footsteps?
I think if it's in you to write, you will write. It's a sort of natural compulsion. The good news is that, while publishing deals are

always elusive, there are many markets out there for writing – and many ways to be a writer. The internet has opened up massive opportunities for people to reach an audience through personal websites, blogs and networking communities. Some publishers keep a close eye on the net for signs of talent!

There are creative writing courses and degrees up and down the country, which can inspire or maybe buy you the time to get your brilliant work finished. And there are lots of annual competitions to enter. So take a deep breath, begin, explore, develop, keep your spirits up (despite rejections), be exciting, brave, persistent and very flexible. Keep the *Writers' and Artists'* Yearbook by your side for advice, contacts in the industry and submission guidelines. And good luck!

Watch out for more stunning fiction from Jill Hucklesby. Coming Soon!

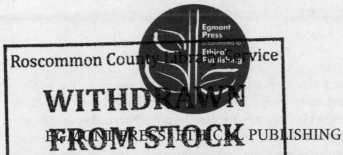

EGMONT PRESS: ETHICAL PUBLISHING

Egmont Press is about turning writers into successful authors and children into passionate readers – producing books that enrich and entertain. As a responsible children's publisher, we go even further, considering the world in which our consumers are growing up.

Safety First
Naturally, all of our books meet legal safety requirements. But we go further than this; every book with play value is tested to the highest standards – if it fails, it's back to the drawing-board.

Made Fairly
We are working to ensure that the workers involved in our supply chain – the people that make our books – are treated with fairness and respect.

Responsible Forestry
We are committed to ensuring all our papers come from environmentally and socially responsible forest sources.

For more information, please visit our website at www.egmont.co.uk/ethical

Mixed Sources
Product group from well-managed forests and other controlled sources
www.fsc.org   Cert no. TT-COC-002332
© 1996 Forest Stewardship Council

Egmont is passionate about helping to preserve the world's remaining ancient forests. We only use paper from legal and sustainable forest sources, so we know where every single tree comes from that goes into every paper that makes up every book.

This book is made from paper certified by the Forestry Stewardship Council (FSC), an organisation dedicated to promoting responsible management of forest resources. For more information on the FSC, please visit **www.fsc.org**. To learn more about Egmont's sustainable paper policy, please visit **www.egmont.co.uk/ethical**.

D0274154

Breathe. Stand still. Blend in. Don't cough.
Shhh, heart. Don't beat so loud . . .